I dedicate this book to God, my daughter Jaz, and everyone who believed in me.

Street Ink Publications
P.O. Box 231051
Det., MI. 48223
WWW.Streetinkbooks.com

Thanks to my dudes at Ryan Corr. Fac. In Detroit, D.X. (D. Snead) for the cover art & Dr. Islam for the scientific research and author, Stephen Geez, for helping me get my ink game proper!

1

Drug Lords

by

E. Scrill

Printed in the United States of America

Prologue

Mack watched his friend's dark face form a charismatic smile as Fleetwood stepped out onto the porch.

"What's up, young dog?"

"I was just in the 'hood, so I stopped by. I got some fire." Mack held up a pencil-thick joint.

At thirty-two, Mack was ten years younger than Fleetwood, brown-skinned, and had a face like a black Errol Flynn's. His body was forged to definitude by prison weight pits, chiseled enough to make the prissiest woman want to hump his leg in broad daylight.

"Put it in the air." Fleetwood grabbed a lighter from his pants pocket and flicked flame to the end of the mummy.

Mack puckered up and hit the weed until it became angry-red. He extended an iced-out wrist as Fleetwood pinched the joint from Mack's fingers.

"Damn, gee! You got enough ice on yo' wrist to freeze the African sun." Fleetwood filled a jaw with smoke, and then swallowed it down. "I heard you got a new dope spot bangin' on Clements. Niggas tell me you got the fiends fallin' through like they supposed to." Still holding the indo vapors captive in his lungs, Fleetwood continued. "Just don't forget what I told y'all 'bout stackin' that bread."

Young dog, you can hustle forever, but if you ain't stackin' yo' dough, you just spinnin' yo' wheels, Mack reflected as he grabbed the joint for another pull. He tried to inhale enough tranquility to keep the touchy matter at hand from

3

E. Scrill/DRUG LORDS

racking his brain.

The new virus, ZGP, was killing legions of individuals around the globe, and Mack had enough of the new cure to save just one person. How could he possibly choose who to save and who to let die? He never thought of that problem when wishing for the medicine. But now, with it in his hands, he decided to deal with those who had long money.

His homie, Big Stan, had pockets that were pregnant with drug money, and claimed to be experiencing dreadful symptoms. Fleetwood didn't have ZGP, but his sister was definitely doomed by the virus.

Fleetwood had taught Mack most of what he knew about the streets, and had been in the dope game before Mack knew what pussy was.

By the time the joint was a roach, Mack decided to roll with his first mind since he knew Fleetwood's sister would be a stinking cadaver within the next six weeks if he didn't help her.

"What's on yo' mind, young dog?" Fleetwood asked.

"I was thinkin' 'bout when I saw you and Sheila a few months ago. How is she?"

"Man, she hangin' on. I really hate to see her like that, too. In a way, I wish she would just let go and end it all." Fleetwood looked down to his slippers. "Why don't you come in and see her for yourself?" he asked, pulling open the screen door, allowing Mack to step into the house.

As Mack walked through the living room, he scoped out pictures of Sheila on the mantle. She was fine as hell, just like he remembered her before he got locked up two years ago.

He dragged his feet through the dining room and thought of the nightmarish apparition Sheila had been reduced to when he saw her last. Mack and Sheila were the same age, but when he saw her last she looked to be eighty-years-old, slumped-over, and skinny as an anorexic crackhead.

His heart somersaulted in his chest as he approached the closed bedroom door.

4

E. Scrill/DRUG LORDS

"Gon' on, open the door," Fleetwood urged.

Like a young boy investigating sex sounds coming from his big sister's bedroom, Mack cracked the door ever-so-slightly. He held his breath, anticipating the scent of hospital sterilization. A chubby caretaker nodded off in a magazine while a ceiling fan buzzed circulation. Forcing his eyes to the bed next to her, he saw a clear, liquid-filled bag dangling from a metal stand. A thin tube snaked from the bag and disappeared into a bony arm that stuck out from under a tomb of white linen.

Mack turned and met Fleetwood's eyes. He breathed, and then turned his eye back to the hairline crack in the door.

Fuck! Mack thought as Sheila's skeletal face scared his high away. A chill snowboarded down his spine. Her eyes looked too large for their sockets, as if they were about to pop out and roll down her face. Mack's body was in a hypnotic freeze.

As Sheila inhaled through her mouth, he imagined her breathing to sound like Darth Vader's. Her coated tongue flicked frothy spittle over her dry lips. Mack shook out of his trance and turned to Fleetwood. "Dig this shit: I think I can help her. I got a plug on the cure for that shit."

Fleetwood's eyes grew large with excitement. "Man, you bullshittin'?" He scanned Mack's face, possibly for signs of trickery. "What's the ticket? We need that shit yesterday!"

"Five gees'," Mack said. He knew he could get more, but wasn't trying to fleece the dying. He planned to deal with paid individuals because he knew they were less likely to run their mouths.

Fleetwood cheesed like he just squoze Alicia Keys. "I'll be right back!" He spun and sprinted through the kitchen. Mack could hear his houseshoes slap every step going to the basement. Two minutes later, he returned with a colossal bankroll.

"That was quick," Mack smiled.

"No time for games, young dog," Fleetwood huffed.

5

E. Scrill/DRUG LORDS

Mack handed over the medicine, and then filled Fleetwood in on dosage intervals.

Fleetwood's eyes pooled with watery praise. "Damn, man, I thought I lost my baby. Mack, you somethin' else. You know how many people you can save with this shit?"

"Yeah, I been thinkin' 'bout it."

"Young dog, let me work this bag wit' you. I'm too old to keep takin' penitentiary chances with that blow. You know you gon' make a mint. Just let me middleman some shit."

Mack looked into the older hustler's expectant eyes, and knew he was dead serious. Fleetwood had been paying his dues to the streets forever, and now he expected to reap some of the benefits from the seedlings he planted and watered with his game.

He taught Mack everything from ways to elude five-o while slangin' rocks, to flawless techniques that had young Mack getting suckjobs from hood rats. Mack knew the streets would have been a cranky bitch without 'ol Fleetwood arming him with a mental cache' of mind-boggling tactics to slay the pockets of dopefiends and elevate to baller status.

Now, Mack's mentor was merely asking his former pupil for permission to dip a stale crust in the leftover gravy after Mack feasted on the succulent steak. Mack never even thought of forming a team to push the antidote. But, who could refuse a gutter-guru like Fleetwood?

"Dig this," Mack began. "I only got what I gave you right now, but I'm workin' on more. If I can get this shit flowin', I'm definitely gon' put you down."

Disappointment veiled Fleetwood's face. "Aw, man, you gon' spin off ol' Fleet? Young dog, I know a tycoon like you probably got a warehouse of this shit." Fleetwood stopped talking and slowly shook his head while maintaining a frown, performing his hardship with full ceremony.

Aw shit, not the guilt trip! "Man, you know I wouldn't play you like that. That ain't even for us."

"I ain't think so, but…"

6

E. Scrill/DRUG LORDS

"Straight up, playa, I'm gon' holla soon as," Mack said while turning toward the front door, leaving Fleetwood looking shot-down.

Chapter 1

"Stop calling here, you fucking whore! You burnt my dick!" Dr. Fluellen's deep voice went tenor as he vented his anger over his cordless phone. He perched atop his porcelain throne, pissed because his asshole was sore and feeling raw from his constant diarrheic episodes. He was certain that Melinda, his neighbor, was where he acquired the ZGP virus that had him suffering. She was his only sexual outlet in the three year period after his wife left.

Melinda was a reputed barfly who lived with her mother a few doors down from Dr. Fluellen in a beautiful, subdivided area of Stone Mountain, Georgia. At the age of 38, her once pretty face was ruined from excessive alcohol abuse, causing her to look 10 years older. Her voice was rough and words slurred even when she was sober. She still had a body that would leave most video vixens inferiorly complexed, and pulled no punches when she sicked her veteran coochie on the rebounding doctor, opening his nose wide enough to move her suitcases into.

"Damn, damn, damn," Donyale shouted as he slammed

the phone against the floor. *If Pat was still here, everything would be ok,* he thought. He rested his chin on his fist, thinking back to when life was good, when he had a family. His dedication to his career at the Center for Disease Research (CDR) left his wife lonely, so she bounced, influencing their 17 year-old daughter to join her in Detroit. After that, Donyale drank himself into a stupor each day after work.

Donyale was one of the few African-Americans that ever were the head of a team of biochemists. They were working on a cure for the recent mutation of the Zestora virus. The new virus, having just evolved in the last four years, seemed impervious to all the team's attacks. Even Zyproxo, the strongest antibiotic known to man, had no effect on the new strain.

Its new name, Zestora Gram-Positive (ZGP), has become synonymous with death, killing much faster than cancer. It is transmitted by the exchange of bodily fluids. Once acquired, it attacks the central nervous system. No infected human has survived more than six months. Under high-power microscopes, Donyale's team witnessed the virus attack a pair of streptococcus bacteria, giving the pathogens its own DNA structure

The infected bacteria was stained with crystal violet then treated with an iodine solution, decolorized with alcohol, and counterstained with safranine. Though infected, the bacterium was still gram-positive, meaning it had retained the stain from the crystal violet.

The team began experimenting with different nucleoside derivatives at that point. That's when Melinda became harder for Donyale to find, and his drinking kept his blood-alcohol level above average.

While on the way to work one morning, Donyale called himself taking a few sips from his gin bottle. But, by the time he reached downtown Atlanta he had drained the whole pint.

He continued with his daily routine, contrary to the advice of several of his team members who smelled his toxic breath. He screwed up while mixing chemicals and caused a phosphorus combustion. The fire resulted in thousands of dollars worth of ruined equipment, along with the loss of countless man-hours of research. He was immediately terminated and escorted from the premises by armed guards.

Donyale looked around his basement laboratory, frustrated by his mediocre equipment. But, he knew he had to get back to work. His time was ticking away, and soon he would be too sick to try to find a cure himself. Luckily, he maintained the back-up computer files of his team's research prior to his termination. He knew that with those files he was ahead of the game, and if his old team did find a cure, he wouldn't be able to get down. It would be available only to certain dignitaries like every other virus they had cured.

Chapter 2

Mackenzie Sutton hopped from the air conditioned bus into the blinding rays of the May sun. He crossed McNichols, and started the two block journey to his home. Dressed in the lame, tan outfit he was released from prison in, he didn't care who saw him walking or riding the iron pimp; he was just glad to be free and on the west side of Detroit again. As he strolled down the first block, he thought back to the last time he walked these streets. A new set of kids now ran wild in the 'hood. Mannish boys jumping curbs on their bikes, while others engaged in games of hide-and-go-get-it with curious girls of their age bracket. He felt as if this 'hood had always been his, filled with memories everywhere he turned, from backyards he infiltrated to steal fruit from trees, to the house with the cockblocking poodle across the alley that relentlessly yapped while he stood behind the garage and received his first kiss.

As a child, these brutal streets raised him and gave him a greater sense of security than his own home, where abusive wolves preferred their privacy in order to exhaust his drunken mother both sexually and financially.

Mackenzie walked past the decrepit house where his

old friend, Johnny once lived, remembering the first mission they went on.

John Dollar, as Mackenzie called him, had his back when Ninean, Mackenzie's younger sister was raped. One of their mother's predatory boyfriends noticed Ninean's breast beginning to bud. The drunk and musty brute pulled a hymen heist, causing serious damage to her uterus. The physician's prognosis was that she may never be able to reproduce. The authorities were informed, but their mother covered for her boyfriend, allowing him to escape prosecution. Ninean was sent to live with their father.

Ninean's removal from the home was not nearly enough for young Mack, as Johnny called him. The teenage hoodlums devised a plan that broke his mother's heart.

They abducted the culprit at gunpoint as he staggered from a liquor store. Using a stolen car, they drove him to an abandoned house where they beat and tortured him. Mack placed all blame on the rapist for everything that was ever done to his family by men like him, while driving rusted screws through his hands and feet. His high-octave screams and pleas for help went unheard as the final screw went through his ball sac. John Dollar and Mack torched the car as well as the house containing the bloody corpse, erasing all evidence linking them to the crime.

Even back then, the two possessed talents that rivaled those of Copperfield's; able to make a nigga vanish into thin air. When crack cocaine began to infest the ghettos, the two of them would kill at the request of older drug dealers for as little as an ounce of "hard". The drugs received for payment put young Mack into the dope game.

Mack stood in front of his two-story brick home. Ninean lived there while he was locked up. He let her live with him after the death of their father five years ago. His only rule was that she could never bring men to the crib. Mack had too much blingin', baller shit to have niggas fallin' through. Ninean proved to be very helpful to him by keeping the place up or running errands if he was too busy with other things. She was an excellent cook, therefore, he kept the kitchen stocked with groceries so she could throw down as much as she liked.

He never told her when he was getting out, thinking that if she was having guys over, he would be able to pop-up and catch her in the act. Loyalty was very important to him. Deep down, he was hoping that she would pass the test.

Ninean had rearranged the furniture, but he didn't care, he was just glad to be home. Seeing that she was gone, he quickly shucked his state rags, showered, then dressed in a fresh shorts outfit. When he slipped on his diamond pinky ring with matching ear bling, he felt charged with the vivacity of a true baller. He pawed through the frozen goods in his freezer, looking for his stash of primo weed. Finally, he found his treasure in the bottom corner just were he left it, well preserved in an old peanut butter jar.

Mack climbed into his Yukon Denali, praying that his sister had followed his instructions and drove it every once in a while to keep it operational. When he turned the key, a smile curved his mouth as the engine jumped to life.

Mack bounced through the 'hood, never stopping to kick it, just tapping his horn. He felt like the other hustlers were glad that he took a fall since it freed up lots of customers for everyone else. He knew that would all change now that he was out. He had plans to pass them all up again, taking the game farther than he ever had before. But for now, he wanted to lay up with someone's daughter.

He slowly cruised Belle Isle, watching as the bright rays of the sun seemed to energize everyone. The island park was crowded with people of all ages. The air was filled with the familiar smell of grilled hot dogs and hamburgers. Families were gathered together for picnics and family reunions, couples were spending quality time together, and then there were the thugs, just hangin' out. Even the sea gulls were out wailing while scouring the Isle for discarded foodstuffs. Mack slowed to allow a group of young girls to cross the road to watch a game of hoops. The smell of barbeque invaded his nostrils, bringing back pleasant memories of days when he would contribute slabs of ribs for the annual block club party in the 'hood.

Ignoring a radio warning about the new ZGP virus, Mack popped in a CD. He stuck a joint in his mouth and fired up. The music wasn't very loud, but the bass from his 12-inch speakers caused the images in his rear-view mirror to ripple from the vibrations.

He turned up the sounds and headed for the main strip as he toked on the spliff. He was hoping to run up on some young tenderony who would find herself taken in by his smooth lines and deceitful influence. Knowing himself to have always been a magnet for rubber banded bankrolls and fast women; he knew that some pussy was on the way. He eyeballed conceit in his visor mirror and smiled. Settling in his seat, he felt the euphoric effects of the indo kicking in.

As he crept down the strip past posing wannabees, he found a place to park near some swings. Stroking his chin with his forefinger and thumb, he scoped out a group of females that were kicking it while bay-bays ran wild nearby.

Oh hell yeah! His eyes bucked as a sudden wind quickly lifted the flimsy skirt of one of the females. Trying to hold the skirt down, she looked to see if anyone had noticed what happened. The sight had already been burned into Mack's mind. He fought to keep a straight face as their eyes locked. All the while, he still envisioned the defiant hairs peeking around the sides of the petite, white panties decorated with pink flowers that held her pubic mound captive.

Blushing from embarrassment, deep dimples amped-up the bewitching looks of the fair-skinned woman. Her hair was collected in a neat, long ponytail with soft curls caressing the frame of her forehead. The pink sandals she had on to match her pink skirt set revealed a pair of perfectly manicured toes. Her body was tight and curvy in all the right places. Even

14

without make-up, Mack found the dimepiece monopolizing his attention.   She put her forefinger to her full lips, playfully gesturing for him to keep what he saw a secret.

With his forefinger, Mack called for her to come closer. "Get out," she motioned with her lips. Leaving the truck running, he met her halfway. The other females stared, perhaps with envy as their girl flashed an electric smile while kicking it with the six-foot-two stud.

Mack tried to keep his eyes off her tits. "So what do they call you?"

"Rachel or Ray. What about you?"

"Mack."

"So, is that what you do, just 'mack' all the women?" she joked, staring into his face as if she awaited a clever response.

"Naw, that's not what I'm about. But, if you need me to…" He rubbed his chin, realizing that his time away caused his game to fall off like a bad pack of dope. Before he could utter another word, he noticed that she had become mesmerized by the large cluster of diamonds garnishing his pinky. Each small princess-cut prism exploded with brilliant colors from the red and blue ends of the light spectrum.

"I'm just here to help," he told her. She smiled like she couldn't wait to. "And just what help do you offer, Mr. Mack?" She had a hand on her hip, checking out his muscular frame.

"Depends on what kind of help you need. But for now, just try my friendship."

"I don't know. The name Mack makes you sound like a thug."

"Is that what I look like to you?" He countered, turning both palms upward in an attempt to seem innocent. He knew himself to be the biggest thug around.

Ray looked him over. "Naw, I guess not. I really can't be sure right now. I'll have to see."

"You won't be able to see unless you spend some time

15

with me. Think you can get rid of your friends?"

"Depends. You never did say how old you are."

"That's cause I'm old enough to know it don't matter much. But, if it makes you feel better, I'm thirty-two."

"I'm twenty-one."

Normally, her young age would have made bonin' her seem like overkill to Mack, but she was fine, and he had been gone two long years. His scheming mind was already mapping out the ways he could undermine her will to keep her panties up. "Well, do you drink or smoke weed?"

"See, I knew you was a thug," she smiled. "No, I don't smoke. I need my brain cells for college. Sometimes I might have a little something to drink, though."

"Well, when you shake your girls, call me so we can find a spot to get our sip on." He exchanged numbers and smiles with her, then backed away watching the melodic way her hips rolled away.

* * *

A soothing twilight breeze blew in Mack's open window as he steered through the narrow streets of Rosedale Park, stopping at the address given to him over the phone. The house was not as large as most on the block, but was just as neat. With instructions not to blow his horn, he waited patiently. Moments later, Ray appeared on the side of the house flashing her sparkling teeth. Mack once again ignored a radio warning about the new viral scare, entranced by the way Ray's alluring breasts led her to the SUV.

"Hi," she said, plopping down on the front seat. Her perfume filled the air.

"What's going on, Miss Ray?"

"So, where we headed?"

"I was thinking maybe The Platinum Lounge. The food there is pretty good in case you get hungry."

"I've been there before. It's cool."

Bootsy Collins crooned, "I'd rather be with you" as the

couple coasted down McNichols toward the lounge, which was suggested for its convenience since Mack's three-bedroom home was just a few blocks away.

Inside the small lounge, Mack and Ray sipped Moet mixed with Alize. As soon as a buzz hooded Mack's eyes, he got to blazin' the lame karaoke performers. His eyes were glued to Ray's Coke bottle-shaped body as she walked to the restroom. When she returned, she tried to get past Mack to get to her chair, but he grabbed her arm. Overconfident from the tranquilizing drinks, he pulled her down onto his lap. Her sweet smell and the soft feel of her ass in his lap turned his dick to stone. When he released her, she teasingly grinded herself against his bulge. Ready to put an end to his sexual depravity, he suggested that they take the party elsewhere.

"Where?" she questioned.

"Let's get some drinks and go to my crib. I'm sure we can find somethin' on cable to watch us."

"Might as well. Nothin' else to do but go home and listen to my ex beg me to get back with him. He know I don't have school, so he tries to hang around to make sure I don't see nobody else."

Ray had grown tired of her boring relationship with Damon. Feeling it was necessary, she gave her high school sweetheart his walking papers. He wasn't maturing or coming through like her friend's older boyfriends with fancy purses or shimmering trinkets to adorn her neck and wrist. No, not Damon. Instead of making sure his pockets were lined with cash, he tried to spend all of his time with Ray, which got old really fast. The fact that he was her first was what kept him from getting the boot sooner.

She had been reluctant to give herself to anyone else for fears that they, too, might turn out to be a loser, seeking only to torpedo her amateur crevice, and then wind up being more fatal than Damon. So, she allowed him to linger for company, and if he had protection, her intermittent sexual itches.

Mack was glad to hear her opening up, giving him much needed info to manipulate the situation. "You know you love that nigga."

"Naw, we past that now. I do still care for him, though."

"You must've put it on him for him to be actin' like that. Don't get me caught up in no love triangle," he teased.

After stopping at the store for drinks, Mack backed his truck into his backyard, not really planning on leaving again that night. In the silence of the night, horny crickets could be heard strumming love ballads as Mack led his curvaceous guest through his side door.

Mack sat on his living room sofa, sucking on a joint, watching Ray as she checked out the photos on the mantle. He mixed drinks for the two of them, making hers extra strong. When she bent over to grab her drink, her shirt sold her out like her skirt had earlier, revealing precious cleavage. They sipped and chatted after finding nothing worthwhile to watch on television. The more Ray sipped, the harder she laughed at Mack's jokes. That let him know she was about ready.

"When do you go back to school?" he inquired.

"I got homesick at Ferris, so this fall I'm going to Wayne State."

"That's good. That means I can still see you when classes start," he said to strangle any inhibiting thoughts she might have of him not calling after getting the ass.

"I guess so. I still can't believe you don't have a woman or a baby momma."

"I haven't been that lucky yet. Maybe I was saving myself for you."

"Yeah, right! You can save the game, young Mack."

Young Mack?

Mack forgot that Ray had just checked out his pictures and took the comment as a slip of her tongue, never acknowledging it, but thinking that one of Ray's girlfriends must have told her about the vast amounts of cash he was alleged to have accumulated during his reign in the streets. That put him at ease, since now he thought that he was already accepted by Ray as the thug that he was. Her being there at that hour, with knowledge of that, could only mean that she was willing to co-star in one of the many sexual fantasies that projected themselves into the theater of his mind every night during his incarceration.

Enveloped in lust, memories flashed of the sassy gyration of Ray's soft ass in his lap, and of the panty-shot allowed to him by her windblown skirt. "Why don't you sit over here?" he asked while stretching his arm across the top of the couch.

Ray nestled up next to him, resting her head on his arm that now wrapped around her. With the hand of the arresting arm, Mack began massaging the contours of Ray's breasts. Her nipple perked in his palm. His other hand set her drink on the coffee table in front of them. As he settled back beside her, he placed his free hand on her knee, sliding it up toward her inner-thigh. With smooth, dithered motions his hand politely ascended up her soft thighs, stopping every few inches to draw small circles with the forefinger before continuing on its mission. She placed her right leg over his left, giving his hand the green light to venture further on his course. Ray gasped as Mack's adept fingers skated over her damp crotch, and then began down inside her undies, stopping to playfully dally in the soft patch of mingled hairs. She moaned his dick stiff as his skillful finger finally entered her. With one hand filled with a buoyant breast, and the other gently stroking her creamy, she went to work on her earlobe with his lips.

He was loving her reactions to the things he was doing to her. He never before bothered with foreplay, never even cared if the woman he was with enjoyed herself--he just stuck it in.

Ray's breathing became more ragged as she began moving her hips upward to meet the rhythm of Mack's fingers.

E. Scrill/DRUG LORDS

She began to shudder, letting him know that a delicious orgasm had surged through her.

Mack removed his slick fingers before suggesting that they go upstairs to his room where they would be more comfortable. He had a tent in his pants thinking of how he got her off. His hooded eyes looked up at Ray, who was now standing in front of him, waiting to be led to his bed.

Chapter 3

After a grueling battle with the toilet, Donyale dialed Melinda's number.

"Hello..." a female voice answered.

"Yes, this is Donny. Is Melinda there?"

"Oh, Dr. Fluellen! I have been desperately trying to reach you. Melinda has been delusional, saying that she was visited by her dead father. She is running a temperature of a hundred-four. I was hoping that you may have some kind of help for my daughter, her being a close friend of yours and all. Please, Donny, she may be entering the terminal stage of the virus any day now."

Donyale knew that the women on the phone spoke the truth. He just hoped he wasn't too late.

After adding hydroxylamine to his prior nucleoside experiment and parlaying it into a satisfactory compound, Donyale tested the concoction on a small monkey he bought at a pet store and injected with the virus. Seeing that the monkey's appetite had increased after a week, he checked the mitosis of the small mammal. Its cells no longer divided unevenly, meaning that his potion was working.

He tested his own temperature, and had reached a

21

scorching 100 degrees. Plagued by grisly visions of becoming a dead body before the monkey could fully recover, he decided to test his findings on the source of his infection. He hated to rush and do anything out of haste, but his ass was on the line.

"Look, I'll be over tonight," he said into the phone. "Don't inform anyone of her condition, I just may be able to save her."

Using supplies he copped from on old schoolmate who was now a pharmacist, Donyale made capsules from the ingredients in his crucible which he ground into powder. He knew that those antibiotics may be the only hope for thousands, or even millions. He tossed a few dozen pills into a plastic baggy and headed for Melinda's.

He was met with the respect of a king as he instructed Melinda's mother to administer one capsule, three times a day with food. After being sworn to Illuminatic secrecy, she stashed the pills in her bedroom.

"Did you ever take her to get medical attention?" Donyale asked after noticing Melinda's deteriorated condition as she lay in her bed on the borderline of consciousness.

"She hasn't been to a doctor since she found out what was causing her headaches and indigestion. We were going to go in the next few days if we couldn't contact you."

"If she doesn't improve in the next week, call me. Matter of fact, if the symptoms persist after the next few days, call me." *Hopefully, it works. If not, too damn bad. The whore probably knew she had the shit when she gave it to me,* he thought coldly. He felt better since he had given the guinea pig its first experimental dose.

Now was the waiting period. He was a suffering, shitty mess while waiting to see if he had successfully resurrected Melinda.

He knew he wouldn't have time to watch for side-effects. For all he knew, a third arm could sprout from a person's back, but if it allowed them the chance to live longer, he would crank out as many capsules as he could.

E. Scrill/DRUG LORDS

The week was crawling by so slowly that Donyale thought his calendar was broke. To keep busy, he stayed on the grind making more capsules. After popping two aspirins for his migraines, he reached for the phone to call his daughter.

"Hey, how you doin'?" he said to his ex-wife who answered the phone.

"Hello, Donny. Have you been feeling any better? I sure hope you are doing better than me. I think I may have contracted that new virus."

"What makes you say that?" he quizzed, happy to hear that his ex was suffering.

"Well, I have a painful lump in my armpit, and my bowels have been runny for the last month or so."

"What about the guy you're seeing? Does he have any symptoms?" He almost drooled as his mouth hung open while anxiously awaiting the answer. He was almost certain that she got burned by his successor, and would only be able to right herself by crawling back to him--the one she called a boring lab rat and left behind. She knew he had been sick, but didn't know he had the virus. He sure as hell wasn't going to tell her, either.

"You must be talking about Dale. Well, we called it quits about a month and a half ago."

"So, how's my baby doing?" He asked, satisfied to hear that his baby momma was alone during her trying times. He knew that she was well aware that if she had stayed with him, he would have rode with her till the end.

"She's doing fine. She isn't here, though."

"Oh yeah, she's probably with that guy she went to the prom with." He hoped the good-girl images he had of his daughter were still accurate.

"Oh no, she isn't seeing him anymore. I thought he was such a nice young man, too. But, I try not to interfere with her life."

He thought for a minute about his daughter. How she must have matured since he saw her last over a year ago. He

23

missed them both, but at least he did have a good relationship with them. He just prayed that his daughter wouldn't slip up and fall into the clutches of one of those fast talking street niggers and jack-off her good upbringing.

As soon as he hung up the phone, it rang.

"Hello?"

"Hey, Donny! What's up, baby?"

"Melinda! I see you're doing better." The liveliness in her voice sent a rainbow of joy through him. She sounded better, which meant he had struck gold.

"Yeah, thanks to my guardian angel. My mother told me how you came to my rescue. Thanks. I owe you big time!"

"Don't worry about it. What are friends for?"

"Cut the shit. You saved my life. You just wait till I get better…you can do whatever you want--"

"So, your fever and diarrhea are gone?" he interjected.

"Well, the diarrhea is, but my temp is down to a hundred."

"Stay off the booze. It will interfere with the medication. And whatever you do, don't tell anyone what happened. Please!" He had been thinking of the loose lips most females have. "I guess I did kind of save you, so…you owe me."

"Now the man is coming out of you," she said, smiling with her words.

"Well no. What I need for you to do is to promise me that you won't tell a soul that I helped you. No matter how much another person may mean to you, I won't be able to help them. So, it's no use letting the cat out of the bag."

"The cat ain't out the bag yet! Just wait till I get better, I'm gonna show you--"

"Just promise me. Can you please do that?"

"Okay, I promise. Why are you so uptight, anyway?"

"I'm all right. I just need to take care of myself now, that's all."

Silence persisted for a full minute. "I'm sorry, Donny. I-I forgot…"

"Don't worry about me; I told you, I'll be all right." He dropped the phone onto the base, then headed for the lab, taking three steps at a time. He looked at his watch, then took the first capsule.

*   *   *

After a week and a half of taking the new antibiotic, Donyale began feeling like himself again. He sat Melinda down with the ingredients to make more capsules, and schooled her for several hours before he felt confident that she could handle the task on her own. With his creation in production, he decided to pay his daughter a visit.

He couldn't wait to see his suffering ex. He even thought about allowing her to hurt until she teetered on the brink of death before he helped her. But, he knew if she died, then his daughter wouldn't have a mother. He just hoped Melinda would stay off the bottle so that she could recover and keep pumping out capsules. She was the best person to help since she knew the stuff existed. He just needed to make it clear to her that she would never again get his dick in her hand. He had lost his appetite for her completely.

Chapter 4

Ray was completely lost in Mack's muscular embrace. She had never been so turned on in her life. Mack's muscles worked like a mojo, and seemed to strike her shameless. She would have never believed that she would hook up with someone that much older than her. But, Mack was talking good, and was handling the situation like it was all supposed to be happening. She just met him earlier that day, and already she had allowed him to smooth off her clothes; something that took Damon two years to do. She wanted to be totally submissive with him.

He stood behind her in his red boxers after dropping her skirt to the floor. He lightly traced her navel with a finger, awakening snoozing goose bumps. She tilted her head to allow the sugary kisses he planted on her neck and shoulder. His graceful hands caressed their way to her back. He stole her bra with the finesse of a booster. Ray purred as he cupped both breasts and maneuvered his tongue about her skin.

She rolled her eyes around under the lids as he began teasing her stiffened nipples with an ascending succession of fingers before sliding slower, moving past her waist, taking down her saturated panties. She leaned back into some serious wood.

He navigated her to an island of a bed before hovering over her, introducing his tongue to her nipples. Pleasure sedated her facial muscles. She knew that if he were to stop, she would abandon all of her principles and beg him to break her off properly.

Damn, it feel like he's going up into my stomach.

"Go slow," she pleaded. Ray held Mack in a death grip as he plunged deeper and deeper into her with each stroke. Blissful tears streamed from her eyes as he gripped her ass and humped her with jackrabbit vigor. His magic wand seemed to sweep every nerve ending inside her, sending powerful climaxes surging through her. Her ears filled with Mack's bellowing moan as she felt his seed splash inside her.

The two fully spent lovers clung together like Velcro as they embraced passionately.

Ray flashed on her times getting down with Damon; they were child's play compared to the way Mack handled his biz. She almost got pissed thinking of all she missed wasting time with him. As she drifted off to dreamland, she smiled, thinking of the way she had been KO'd by cupid.

Ray awoke the next morning still clinging to Mack's body. She cursed herself for giving it up so soon; she knew she should've stood her ground. But she wanted to so bad that she just couldn't say no; he was so smooth and sexy; plus she was drunk. She wondered how things would end up, if she would hear from him again.

God knows she wanted to.

*   *   *

After watching Ray disappear into her house, Mack decided it was time to dig up some of his old connects so he could get grindin' again. The problem was, while watching the news in the joint, he saw so many people that he knew get killed or indicted that he didn't know who he could trust to cop from. For all he knew, all of his old plugs could be hot.

E. Scrill/DRUG LORDS

He finally reached Duke, the nephew of his old supplier and homeboy, Big Stan.

Stan pushed *much* powder, slangin' nothing less than an eighth of a kilo. He had the Herman Gardens housing projects completely sold-up in his teenage years when he flipped rocks and half-tracks. Later, he graduated to moving weight, known for the best Peruvian flake on the west side of Detroit. He had also exceedingly contaminated the city with his offspring, having more than fifteen sniveling crumb snatchers by twelve different women, all with his round jowls, large ears, and over-sized feet.

"Where's Stan?" Mack inquired.

"He's out shopping," Duke began, "for something to wear to J.D. 's funeral. He died from that new ZGP shit. It's been wiping' niggas out!" He paused to yell something to someone in the background. "When did you get home anyway?"

"I just got back. Listen, how long did he have it?" Mack had seen the reports and news stories, but didn't think it would actually touch the 'hood for some time.

"Man, he just found out three months ago. He didn't know what was causin' his diarrhea, thought it was all the drinkin'. Found out way too late. You should have seen him, man. He woulda loved to have had HIV instead."

"The shit is like that?"

"Hell yeah! People been out here dyin' like they pissed me off or somethin'."

"Like they pissed you off, huh?" Even with the sad event looming, Mack had to take time to laugh at that one; he knew Duke was soft as squid pussy.

"But for real, it's been like Revelations in the Bible or somethin'. So, when you creep wit' them freaks, you better strap-up; you never know when that thang is rotten, she might not even know."

Mack swallowed hard, thinking of the night before. What if Ray was out there bad? An image flashed in his mind

28

of Lucifer, twirling the end of his pointy mustache with an evil grin after baiting Mack into the graveyard with a young dime piece that seemed to have low mileage.

Mack had rubbers, too, but Ray's bewitching splendor pulled him in raw. He knew that while he was locked up, the possibilities for that happening with a bad bitch like her were endless. At least HIV would give him two more years, but he had been hearing that the time frame for ZGP was like six months--max! He wished he could rewind time and go back to before he let his other head call the shots. He had let his dick take charge, and possibly set himself up for the worst. It seemed bold as hell to just get out, knock off a rotten broad, and be dead before New Year's Day. *Sonuva bitch!*

After being briefed on funeral arrangements, Mack decided to get fresh, too. He knew he would run into everybody he needed to at the funeral, and nobody wanted to deal with a nigga looking like yesterday. He also planned to take a burner. He knew people he had fucked over would figure him weakened by his bit, and might pounce in the name of revenge.

He hit Fairlane Mall, where one of his old customers used to hook him up. In the Broadway, he got laced up with a black short-sleeved shirt with black slacks, then paid a gee for a pair of three-quarter Cayman Crocs with soft alligator-print bottoms.

Stepping through the mall, he ran into dozens of people, all asking where he'd been or when he got out. It felt good to be missed by so many. Some he didn't even recognize, but figured that at one point or another they had been to one of his many money spots.

He had sold everything from raw to trees, sometimes having as many as five spots bangin'. He never chilled at any of them once they got pumpin', he only stopped by to pick up dough and drop off more work--if he didn't have a reliable runner at the time.

Once he got home, he dressed and headed for the small

funeral home on West McNichols, stopping for the light at Hubbell and dropping the truck's visor to shield his eyes from the sun. Cars lined both sides of the busy street, so he knew the parking lot was on-jam. He never counted on the problem of where to park, so he slowly crept by, looking for a vacancy. He spotted a car leaving right in front of the place. This was good in case he got into a beef.

Inside, he was greeted like a ghetto celebrity, most of the hustlers gave him five with cash in their hands, something done to a fellow baller after he got out in case his bit left him on his knuckles. That was a way a hungry hustler could get back on without having to hit licks. Every street nigga doin' dirty deeds knew the joint was waiting, and nobody knew when they, too, might need to get sprinkled.

The chapel was crowded like the county jail bullpen after a holiday weekend. Mack vainly searched for an empty chair, then noticed Ray across the room with her arm around some lame. He acted as if he didn't see her, continuing to listen to the minister preach a fiery sermon about repentance and the last days. From the corner of his eye, he watched her comfort the grieving sucker. His mind drifted back to the night before, how she had nourished his sexual starvation.

He had loved the way she felt and smelled cuddled next to him, definitely better than the hard-ass jail house bed with the stagnant fumes rising from his bunky underneath. He couldn't help but think that if he wasn't who he was, he may never have even got a shot of that ass. Still, he knew he should never look back, just like he had in the past. He knew it should be easy to smother the memories of Ray with new adventures with freakier ho's. It bothered him, though, the thought of always having to keep shakin' and rollin', never kickin' back with a piece of his own. He felt himself getting older, changing.

Just as he had changed his style of dress from jeans to casual, he planned to somehow change the way he made his cash. The transition that started during his incarceration now made him different, not only from who he used to be, but from his old homies as well. He knew he would always be a hustler, forever warped by the streets, but now he saw the world through more mature eyes; no more the eyes of a knuckle-headed savage. For this, he was glad to have been gone. He could never fully return to his old ways.

He glanced at Ray again, thinking about how the fool next to her probably thought she was all his. He would definitely need someone to comfort him if he knew what she did last night. *That's why I never trusted bitches.*

Mack tried not to think so much of her pouting soup coolers, the way they felt kissing him; of her epic peaks, the way they bounced when he rode her; of her snug sugar walls that caused him to lose his composure and make retarded noises as she milked his balls. He knew it was a good thing he had seen this since a round two with the dime piece crossed his mind.

As the crowd thinned, he watched a few break to the restrooms. He went out front to kick it with some of the fellas, who put him up on nightmarish ZGP tales.

"Mack," Ray said, surprising him from behind.

He ignored her.

"Hel-lo," she sing-songed.

He turned and faked, "Oh what's up Ray? What you doin' here?"

"I came with my ex. J.D. was his cousin. I knew he would take it pretty hard, so I kinda wanted to be here with him."

"Well, dig that. That's real sweet; I wish I had somebody to comfort me in tryin' times."

"Cut it out! I don't even mess around with him no more. You didn't ask me to come here with you, did you?" Ray folded her arms and twisted her glossy lips. She looked at Mack as if she had made a valid point.

"I just found out today."

"So, I guess I'll hear from you later?" she asked.

E. Scrill/DRUG LORDS

"That must be Damon…Damn, he look pissed. You better get in yo' place."

"I ain't got no place!" Ray retorted, whirling around to meet an angry Damon storming toward her.

Mack watched as Damon and Ray began arguing. A small crowd of the remaining guys found Damon's cross examination entertaining, adding their oohs whenever Ray checked out on him. Mack and Stan stood together.

"Damn, you gon' take that shit, nigga?" Stan began. "I would *never* let no bitch talk to me like that, 'specially in public." He had already caught wind that Mack was doin' Ray.

Damon got pumped up from the jeers and comments. "Fuck it then, bitch! I hope that nigga give you that ZGP shit and make yo' ass curl up and die! I knew I shoulda *been* bounced on yo' ass," Damon spat, trying to put his mack hand down.

"Well that's cool," Ray began with icy stability as she took the stage. "I hope you remember that when you call tonight, beggin' me to get back with you."

*　　　　*　　　　*

Damon short-cut across the well manicured lawn of the funeral home to his compact car; he knew he had fucked up.

She had come with him to make him feel better, but he was ambushed by jealousy when he saw her up in the other guy's face. He didn't even know if the other guy was trying to squeeze her; he just knew he no longer had her heart shackled. He had planned to put on a watery, Oscar-caliber performance with hopes of tugging her emotions enough to get his dick wet. Now he knew it would be no get-back for him, all that precious energy put into the relationship…in vain.

He peeped to see if maybe she was looking his way, but she was still there, gettin' squoze. How desperately he wanted to run back to her and beg for forgiveness, but his mile-high fence of pride was holding him captive, keeping him from doing anything but watching the scene through the blurred vision of his teary eyes. He put his car in gear, slowly pulling off, knowing from her words that he had jacked-off any chances for phone justice later, feeling deep within his gut that anything they once had was history.

Damon wished he had a magic lamp. He would stroke the damn thing until his fingerprints rubbed off, just to get the genie to send him back in time. Back to the wonderful days when Ray would kiss and cling to him possessively, granting him fondlings that one day led to him bustin' her out. The onslaught of Damon's emotions burst his optical dams, sending salty rivers dribbling off his chin and onto his shirt.

R. Kelly's "When a woman's fed up..." played over the radio and twisted the blade that skewered Damon's heart.

He felt like a played-out player.

*   *   *

Mack gazed at Ray's fine ass in her hip-hugging dress while she waited for Damon's mother to give her a ride home. He started to offer her one himself, but knew he would only pit stop home to toss her again. He knew she was watching, so he turned away from her and continued to kick-it with some of the late stragglers. He got Stan's number along with two hundred dollar bills.

"Hit me up later; I got somethin' for you," Stan began. "I know you ready to get busy." He headed for his Cadillac Escalade.

That was what Mack wanted most, the right plugs to get flowin' again. Other hustlers tried to mash work on him, but he knew he would get more love from Stan. "Cool," he said. "I'll get with you later." Then, before going back to his own truck, he told Ray, "I got a few things to take care of."

Mack counted his chips. He had over twenty-five hundred dollars. Now he wouldn't have to dip into his stash, thanks to the generosity of his homies.

At home, he caught up on current events with his sister before changing clothes, then cut his lawn--something he hadn't done in ages. He would usually just pay a crackhead or some youngster trying to make some change to do the job for him. He swept the remaining grass from the sidewalk and decided to grab a bite to eat before he hollered at Stan.

*   *   *

Marlon Hill had enough of the frivolous beefs with his live-in girlfriend, Angelique. She was the finest woman he had ever been with. She had a smooth, caramel complexion with nice curves shaping her five-foot anatomy. In Marlon's bony embrace, she had to gaze up at his dark face--fouled up by his large flat nose--since he stood five-ten.

He had been on his knuckles since losing his job at the auto plant.

He had made several attempts at slangin' rocks from the side door of their two-family flat, but no one in the Dexter/Davison area would let the "nobody" vamp their clientèle. He needed some muscle. He needed someone who had juice with the other dealers.

As he walked down Davison, he thought about getting another gig, but the light and gas bills wouldn't wait for a legal payday. He needed to make something happen--fast. He didn't have the heart to pull off a robbery or the wit to run a con. That limited his choices to the dope game.

He was already skating on thin ice with hot blades when it came to Angelique. The squabbles became more frequent after losing his job for blazing stones in the bathroom. He hadn't as much as sniffed his live-in poontang in over two months. Getting caught in the basement with the basehead, Cookie, didn't help much. Angelique just went back upstairs, giving him the silent treatment. Feeling the grit-tossing vibes, Marlon opted to take the couch until his boo cooled off. But now, he felt horny enough to give her pussy a black eye.

34

E. Scrill/DRUG LORDS

Knowing she would already be gone if she had the cash or much-needed support from her family and friends, he figured he better lay something down before the lights were out; then he would be hit.

Marlon ducked into a carry-out seafood restaurant to get Angelique's favorite shrimp dinner. He had hopes of gaining some much-needed stripes.

He got in line behind a tall, well-built man he could have sworn was Mack. Marlon didn't see a diamond ring on either of the man's pinkies, nor did he display the crispy-fresh attire Mack was known for. If only he could peep the dude's grill.

When the man approached the counter, the shapely clerk answered Marlon's questions the way she jumped on the man's shit. "What up, Mack?" she said with a foolish, groupie grin.

"How you doin'," he said.

"You don't remember me? Faye, Brandy's friend," she said, flexing her tongue piercing.

"Oh yeah, y'all used to come by the spot and keep me company while I made my dub-sacks. Looks like you put on a few pounds…in the right places."

"You never seemed to notice when you used to take Brandy to the back room and leave me watching the door."

"Hook me up with a fish sandwich and I promise I'll make it up to you."

"I got a man now, but what kind of sandwich you want?"

"Perch. Let me know if your situation changes," he quickly added.

"I'll keep you in mind," she promised, flashing a neon smile.

Waiting for the flirting to stop, Marlon wondered if Mack would remember him. "What's up playa? Where you been?"

Mack turned to face Marlon. "What's up dog? You

35

been alright?"

"Man, I ain't think you was gon' remember me. I just been chillin'. I'm still around on Clements. I know you remember when I used to cut the grass for you," Marlon added on the brown-nose tip.

"Yeah, you was my little mellow. What's been up with you? Still in the landscapin' business?"

"Hell naw! I was workin' at the plant 'till they started hatin' on me."

"May I help you?" the cashier interjected, her wandering eye made Marlon wonder if she was talking to him or Mack.

Marlon gave his order, trying not to stare, thinking of how her eyes seemed to move independently of one another, like one of his refrigerator magnets.

"So you still doin' your thing?" Marlon asked Mack.

"Shit, man, I just got out."

"So you on paper?"

"Naw. I just had to do the two flat for a gun. I'm straight now, though. I'm puttin' a little somethin' together; you know me."

Marlon's heart leaped at his big chance. He knew if he could get down with someone who had a cosmic reputation like Mack, he would be straight. "I'm thinkin' 'bout doin' a little somethin' on the block; you can get down with me if you want."

With Mack, there was no such thing as partners. Every joint venture he engaged in soon became his own solo project…sooner or later. "Well, let me check out the spot so I can see what we're workin' wit."

"You might as well come by the crib with me now. I was just about to take this grub to my woman."

"You and your woman live there?" Mack asked, looking amazed, knowing only dope fiends actually live in the house they work out of, especially if they have a live-in woman. "Let's roll." Mack winked at the cashier as they left, igniting a smile that revealed every tooth in her head. They climbed into the Yukon and jetted from the curb.

Marlon grinned with excitement, thinking of all the possibilities the new spot would create. He wouldn't have to go to others for his drugs now; then there were the ladies who would do anything to get their high on.

His eager grin soon vanished, replaced with the dread of how he would explain Mack's presence to Angelique.

Chapter 5

Angelique went out the side door to take the trash out back to the garbage can, but was startled by two men coming up the driveway. The sun's bright rays kept her from making out who they were, only enabling her to see their silhouettes.

Weasel, one of the men approaching, asked, "Is Marlon home?"

"No. He stepped out for a while," she nervously replied, wondering why they were still heading toward her.

"Well, I'm gon' wait 'til he get back," Weasel began. "He owe me some money and I'm tired of playin' games with him."

Angelique dropped the trash bag and tried to slip back into the doorway, but Weasel's foot stopped the door before she could close it. They then forced their way in.

On the stairway landing, Weasel told her, "Look, I don't want to hurt you. I know you ain't have nothin' to do with him runnin' up a bill with me, but like I said, we gon' wait for him to get back."

Weasel's crony, Jay, pushed past Angelique and started up the stairs, stopping at the door of the first-floor flat.

Jay had met Weasel in the Wayne County jail while

fighting an armed robbery case. On the floor of the day room, the short and chubby Weasel was getting the piss stomped out of him by two inmates he had worked in the streets a year earlier for an ounce of heroin. Jay was on the rock, and already hated the two for squeezing the weak out of their zoom-zooms and wham-whams before he could get to them.

With his over-sized hands clenched into tight fists, the six-two menace leaped to Weasel's rescue, subduing one assailant with a size fourteen to the back. With the wind knocked out of him, dramatic pain creased the assailant's face, and he slowly sank to the floor as if he were melting.

The other inmate was still jitterbuggin' on Weasel's county greens, so Jay bombed him behind the ear with a large ham-hock fist. The dude went limp as an impotent penis, and slept until the deputies came in.

Ever since, Weasel has employed the goon as his enforcer, giving him a better way to make money than stick-ups.

Angelique tried to think of a way to separate herself from the intruders so she could get help. "Where y'all goin'? You might as well wait down here if you don't want to go back outside, that way y'all can see him soon as he get back." She tried to hide her fear, but couldn't keep from trembling. She had never been in a position like this.

That dumb muthafucka! I can't believe he got me in this shit! She often wondered if Marlon was smokin', but now realized that he wouldn't have to run up tabs with dealers unless he had a serious problem. It was time to go since that problem was now jeopardizing her own safety.

"We better wait in the crib with you," Weasel said with a grin that gave Angelique the shivers. "I can't take any chances on you callin' the five-o. Like I said, you'll be safe."

Seeing that it was no other way, she turned and started up the stairs. "That apartment is vacant," she told Jay, continuing to the second story.

Her nervous hands fidgeted with the lock before she

twisted herself into the humble dwelling. An oozing lava lamp sat on a table next to a brown fossil of a sofa. The wooden coffee table was plagued by circular water stains from coasterless beverages. The nappy carpet had a large burn mark, and had definitely seen better days. The dining room's ceiling fan wobbled as it spun, sending the smell of potpourri drifting throughout the home.

"Well, I guess y'all can just wait out here. I'm going in the back to watch some TV," Angelique stated in another attempt to put some distance between her and the lustful eyes that were undressing her.

"Damn, no wonder Marlon kept you a secret. I guess I would too," Jay announced with a sinister grim. "Why don't you just chill out here wit us so we don't get lonely, I would feel a lot better."

*   *   *

As Marlon and Mack pulled into the driveway, Marlon wondered why the trash was just sitting on the side of the house. It was unusual for Angelique to leave the garbage in a spot like that when she knew he would drag his feet cleaning the mess made when strays tore through the bag.

"I'm going to catch this call while you go in and holla at your girl about our hook-up," Mack said as he retrieved his ringing cell phone from his pocket.

"That's cool. I'll leave the side door open, we're on the second floor."

Marlon cat-walked up the steps, listening for anything out of the ordinary. As he neared the door, his heart pounded when he heard what sounded like Angelique in trouble.

He hurried through the unlocked door and found Jay with his arms around a struggling Angelique. Jay had two handfuls of Angelique's large ass as he tried to force her to the couch. He paid Marlon no mind as he groped and violated his woman.

Marlon dropped the food, rushing in to thwart Jay's

attack, but Weasel stepped from behind the door and dropped him with a blow to the back of the head.

"You finally showed up, huh?" Weasel began. "I thought we was gon' have to let your girl work that shit off for you."

Marlon sprang to his feet at the sound of Angelique's shirt being torn, only to be put in a full nelson.

"Since you insist on dodgin' me, run my loot or watch yo' girl give up a little interest on yo' bill."

"She ain't got nothin' to do with this," Marlon began in an asphyxiated tone. "I been workin' on your bread, I just need another week. C'mon, man, let my girl go!"

*   *   *

Jay was oblivious to everything in the room with him except for the curvaceous morsel he struggled to defile. Once he ripped Angelique's bra from her body and freed her luscious breasts, he was like a pitbull that had the taste of blood in its mouth; nothing was going to stop him. *This bitch thick as hell,* he thought as his dick dented his pants from the inside. He handcuffed both her wrists with one of his large hands, stopping her fighting and scratching. With his free hand, he jerked loose the drawstring that held up her jogging pants. "You might like it if you stop fightin'." He puckered his lupine lips and tried to steal a kiss. He found it hard to believe that Marlon could shack-up with a woman like her. "Why can't we be friends? Don't you think I'm a better man than some smoker?" he questioned as he yanked down her pants along with her panties, exposing a cone-shaped, pubic afro.

Marlon's face was scarlet with anger as he helplessly watched his woman being sexually assaulted. She was putting up a much better fight than him, but still seemed to be on the tracks in the path of the train.

"Man, will you stop tryin' to romance her and hurry up! Shit, I'm tryin' to get down, too!" Weasel anxiously said

41

while making sure that Marlon had a good view of the crime. "I'm gon' show you how to hit that shit right," he told Marlon to further his humiliation.

Jay released Angelique's wrists and pinned her legs back so that her knees were pressed against her chest. Her nails raked the skin from his arm. Jay gave her a vicious slap, then captured her legs again, positioning them on his shoulders.

"You gon' make me hurt you. Do that shit again and see what happen," he snarled.

Angelique was defenseless in Jay's monkey-trap. Her face was a mask of horror as he frantically whipped-out his Titanic and prepared to sink it.

*   *   *

Weasel shrugged as he received a stinging slap to the back of his neck. Enraged, he shoved Marlon forward, sending him head-first into Jay, who Marlon grabbed from behind and dragged off the sobbing Angelique.

Weasel about-faced to see who he would punish for the disrespect, but his foot landed on the shrimp dinners, and he slipped up and busted his ass. With his head turned toward the couch, Weasel could see that Jay was thoroughly pissed off having been so close to the moment of truth. Jay's jaw muscles rolled and lumped while he shot venomous eyes at Marlon--at the same time, Jay pulled up his pants to cover his diminishing erection.

Weasel turned to the figure that lurked in the corner of his eye. "Mack! When you get out?" he questioned in disbelief while getting up. "I thought you got about ten years."

"Now you know I'm out, so when you gon' give me that loot you owe me?" Mack said, referring to money from drugs that Weasel received on consignment before Mack's arrest. "I know you got my shit while you and yo' mans here 'bout to run a train on dude's girl--over how much Marlon?"

"A hundred dollars, and he actin'--" Marlon tried to

explain before being cut off.

"A hundred dollars? Damn, consequences get stiff as hell, don't they? Nigga, you owe me five hundred...count it out!"

"Aw, c'mon, dog, that was two years ago--"

"So what you sayin', it ain't my money no more?" Mack's face twisted with fierce contempt. "Nigga, if I do a hundred years, I still want all my loot when I touch down!"

Mack's baritone voice bellowed doom, and every time he raised it, Weasel nearly leaped out of his shoes. Weasel felt like shit having Mack check him in front of everybody. He could feel sweat beads bubbling out of his forehead as he faced Armageddon. He could have sworn he was on top of the situation a minute ago.

Mack straightened his face and in a calm, arctic voice that was lousy with murderous intent, he told Weasel, "Take out the hundred my man owe you, but if you don't have the other four bills in two hours, don't even worry about it."

Weasel knew well that he was getting a break on the hundred dollars, and also that if he didn't get the other four, penalties would be far worse than the tag team they planned to put on Angelique's crevice. "I got you, just come by tonight," he said as he and his crony tried to make an exit.

"Naw, I'm not comin' nowhere," Mack barked. "Did I come to you when you needed that front? Bring that shit by and give it to my man Marlon."

Weasel walked out with his head down, feeling extra crunchy since now he had to scrape up some dough, then check-in with one of his old customers.

*　　　　*　　　　*

Angelique grabbed her torn shirt and headed for the bedroom in the rear of the flat. She wondered who Mack was and what other events would transpire that day. After seeing how he got down, she knew she would be safe on his watch. He had just come from nowhere and bumped Weasel down two levels on the food chain; now he was supposed to give his money to Marlon. Angelique's thoughts and fears all manifested into anger. *Marlon should feel just like a bitch for not being able to save me. I can't believe he still hasn't asked how I am doing. That asshole can stay in there and treat that nigga he with like a god; I'm going to lay down.*

"Are you ok?" Mack asked Angelique as she left the living room. Marlon tried to act on Mack's question and run to check on Angelique, but got a close-up of the door as it slammed in his face. He quickly turned the knob and entered. She sat on the edge of the bed, staring at the floor.

"I'm sorry, baby," he began. "I didn't mean to put you in any danger. You know I care about you."

"You dumb-ass! You smoked-out, now? See, that's real fucked up." Her eyes filled with regretful tears as she thought about the way other guys used to try to lure her into their nest, but Marlon was doing okay at the time, working at the plant. That job went dry as well as the offers from other men.

She looked into Marlon's eyes, piercing his soul. With a clairvoyance of common sense, she knew that a lie was on the way.

"Aw, baby, naw," Marlon began as his eyes fell to the carpet. "Don't believe that shit. You know I wouldn't go out like that."

"Then, why you owe them niggas a hundred dollars?"

"Oh, so you gon' believe them over me?"

"I really don't even care no more."

"Angie-poo. Remember when you used to like me to call you that? Well, anyway, I know it will take a miracle to win your heart back, but I'm not done tryin'.

"I know the timin' ain't right, but I'm 'bout to lay down this little operation with my man in there. I thought you might like to know…that's all. I gotta get on my feet, and that work shit just ain't workin' right now. It will be just for a little while, but if we get hot, you won't get in no trouble 'cause we

44

gon' slang downstairs."

"Marlon, did you see what just happened? It ain't about the police, them niggas will kill you and me! Is your boy gon' be here all the time? 'Cause if not, where will that leave you when the next nigga wanna bust your hard-ass head?"

Marlon looked dumbfounded, staring down at his scuffed gym shoes. "Ain't nobody gon' fuck with us while I got ol' boy with me. You seen how them dudes got up outta here when they seen him. Shit, he didn't have to lift a finger," he plaintively explained, sounding full of hope.

"Sounds like you puttin' too much faith in your homeboy. You do what you want, I doubt if I'll be around to see the next plan backfire in your face," Angelique said in a frustrated tone, thinking of how easy it would be to leave the whole situation if cooked-up 'cain didn't have her father's nose wide open. She put on a shirt and went into the kitchen to get something to drink, trailed by Marlon, still trying to get her to accept his new plan.

"Why don't you just come into the living room and meet him, okay?"

She could feel her eye jumping as her anger neared the danger zone. "Marlon," she began, looking at him as if he offered her used toilet paper in exchange for her soul. "Do you realize what just happened to me? Don't nobody want to meet none of them scantless niggas you fuck wit'!" She retrieved a bottle of rum from the cabinet and took it to the head like a veteran. The deep swallows of the salubrious tonic were supposed to help her relax. She looked at the pint-sized bottle, and doubted that it would be enough to calm her after hearing her man tell her of his new plan.

She began to feel bad for not thanking his friend for defending her honor, because without him… She pushed past Marlon who was just standing there, staring at her behind like a fool, "I hope you get a good daydream, 'cause you won't be touchin' nothin' this way…Dopeman!"

E. Scrill/DRUG LORDS

When she walked into the living room, she was struck speechless as she noticed how handsome Mack was with his widow's peak, smooth brown skin, and oceanic waves flowing through his freshly faded hair. She had to take another hit of the liquid courage before she could speak. "Hi, I just wanted to thank you for steppin' in like you did. I really appreciate your help." *Marlon knows he don't need yo' fine ass up in here around me the way he been fuckin' up!* "Would you like something to drink?"

When Mack looked up to speak, his eyes gripped her and wouldn't let go. It was like a giant hand closed around her, and wouldn't even allow her to turn her head.

"Don't worry about them knuckleheads. I doubt if you have any more trouble outta them. I'm glad I came when I did, though. Marlon's my dog, and you're his woman, so…" Mack stopped as she contorted her face into a humorous frown at the mention of her and Marlon being a couple. "I guess I might as well have a drink," He told Angelique, who was lubricating her esophagus with the booze.

Angelique headed for the kitchen, twisting her hips with the tact of a streetwalker since she could feel Mack's high-beams burning holes in her derrière. She turned the corner and bumped into Marlon, who was apparently being devoured by his insecurities, because he was straining his supersonic ears trying to tap the convo in the next room.

Mack wolfed two glasses of the rum, and then went on a tour of the place with Marlon. He checked the view of the driveway from the window of the stairway landing before they went down to the lower flat.

Inside, the badly stained carpet had the stench of mildew, paintless patches diminished the beauty of the stuccoed ceiling, while a constant dripping echoed from the kitchen. Bars secured the windows that desperately needed new blinds. An old sofa bed, missing the center cushion, sat against the wall in the dining room. They could hear the floorboards creak as Angelique moved about upstairs.

E. Scrill/DRUG LORDS

"This bitch is perfect!" Mack said, looking out the back bedroom window into a fenceless backyard that spilled into a vacant lot, giving clear view to the seafood joint on Davison where he met up with Marlon.

"Yeah, we could have the fiends cut right through that lot into the backyard, then serve 'em from this window," Marlon said.

Mack made a mental note to have the unchecked vegetation cut, knowing its shadows would be a perfect hiding spot for crouching stick-up men. He then checked his watch, remembering the appointment with Stan. "Well dig, I can bring somethin' by later so we can get started."

"Cool, I'm ready whenever you are," Marlon exclaimed.

Mack thought about the roll and how much trouble Marlon could cause, already realizing that he was a smoker. At least he was about to flow again. But, he couldn't figure for the life of him, how Marlon pulled a bad bitch like Angelique.

The red-orange sun began its ceremonious descent behind the horizon as Mack entered the parking lot of the Grandland strip mall. When he opened Stan's passenger door, a thick cloud of smoke poured from the SUV. The aroma stimulated Mack's senses, causing his mouth to water.

He got in and pulled the money out for an ounce of cocaine from his left-front pocket. He had already separated the cash so he wouldn't have to retrieve his pocket's entire contents in front of Stan. He learned years ago that he could forget about bargaining as long as the supplier could see that he had enough to pay full price.

"What up, dog?" Stan said while inhaling from his joint.

"Since when did you get back to smokin' joints? I thought you was a blunt man."

"Well, as strong as this is, you don't need a blunt," Stan exhaled, passing the joint.

E. Scrill/DRUG LORDS

Mack thought of inhaling the new virus from the joint tip that was wet with Stan's saliva. "Naw, I'll wait 'til later when I get my business taken care of. I got this new spot I'm 'bout to crank up. Let me get the circle so I can bounce; it's hot as hell around here," Mack said while looking around for patrolling squad cars.

"Check it out, since you my dog, and I know you gon' get down, I'm gon' throw you another ounce, too. That should get you straight," said Stan.

"Good lookin' out," Mack said, knowing that the extra ounce had nothing to do with friendship, but his ability to flip 'cain. Mack knew Stan was just securing him as a customer, knowing that once he got to runnin' through keys like a locksmith, he would pay for that ounce, then some.

"I'll get with you soon as…" Mack exited the vehicle, and got into his own.

At home, Mack put the two ounces of powder into an empty mayonnaise jar, added the proper amounts of baking soda and water, and then dropped the jar into a pot of boiling water. He waited until the mixture turned into a yellowish, oily-looking blob before taking it from the pot.

He placed the hardening dope on a napkin to cool. He broke a chunk off, weighed it on his triple-beam scale, and then sealed the remainder of the two ounces in a plastic bag, which he stashed in the center of a container filled with corn meal. Taking the grams he separated, he headed for Marlon's.

Chapter 6

Weasel was sick about having the tables turned on him, but there was nothing he could do about it. He had to come up with Mack's cash or he would be a ghost by morning. Worse, he had been belittled in front of his right-hand man, who was probably losing respect for him at that very moment.

He didn't even know where to start. He was broke after the last shakedown from five-o. They took his last three gee's, plus a grand in dope. The conniving bastards even hit him in the stomach, causing him to give up the last meal he had eaten. After that he needed to scrape together dough to cop with, which was his reason for coming down so hard on Marlon. Roughing off Angelique would have been a fringe benefit.

He and Jay cruised while he told Jay that the only way that they would be able to get the money in time would be to hit a lick.

"Well, who do you want to get?" Jay asked, not seeming to mind reaching into his old bag of tricks.

"I don't know, never thought of it 'til now."

"Check it out, I been watchin' these cats over on Strathmoor where I get my trees from. They got the flames,

49

too, one-hitter-quitter," Jay began with a glow in his eyes like he was a mad scientist. "The dude that works the spot is green as hell--a easy mark! He got heat, but never in his hands; it's always on the floor or the table."

Jay began setting the stage for the hold-up, while Weasel's receptive ears absorbed the plan. As the two bolted toward their destination, Weasel was impressed by the goon's cunningness.

Weasel parked his small Dodge on the side street since the spot was two doors down. Next, Jay went in, acting like he was trying to cop.

"Let me see another one, this is too tight," he said, stalling for time.

Weasel knocked twice. As soon as he was let in, he whipped out a chrome nine millimeter and ordered both Jay and the spot worker to the floor.

"Where the fuck is the money and the rest of the weed?" Weasel screamed with maniacal desperation as he administered a kick to the jelly-like abdomen of the mark.

"Man, what the hell you done got me into?" Jay deceitfully asked the overweight victim. "You better tell him, man! That nigga is crazy!"

"The weed is under the couch cushion, and I got the money," the mark answered.

Weasel ordered the fatbody to his knees and rifled through his every pocket before planting a size ten in his back, sending him crashing back to the floor. He then went to the couch and grabbed the drugs, a pistol (which was on the table like Jay said), a stack of CD's, and even the video game system the mark killed time with when shit was slow.

Weasel wrapped the goods in a dirty bed sheet that had covered the sofa. When he ran out the door, Jay got up and ran, too; knowing from experience that if he wasn't there when stolen goods were tallied up, he would get the shit put on him since the guy counting the take would also have been roguish enough to help steal it.

E. Scrill/DRUG LORDS

The two desperadoes sped away with triumphant smiles and adrenaline still pumping.

*　　　*　　　*

Marlon opened the door, rambling on about how Weasel couldn't even look him in the face when he brought the money. "Man, he just threw it down and walked away."

Mack looked him in the face. "And let me guess...you picked it up?"

"Yeah. I ain't care about that, I was just glad to see his face when he brought me the loot."

"I woulda made his ass pick that shit up and put it in my hand. If you don't demand your respect, you don't get none."

"That's true," Marlon agreed, not really heeding Mack's words. "I been lettin' all the fiends know we 'bout to open up. I told 'em we was gon' have the fattest rocks in the 'hood."

Mack sat on two, stacked milk crates, and with surgical precision began dicing the cooked dope into pencil eraser-sized chunks.

Marlon watched Mack work, knowing the size of the stones was larger than average, which would be an important factor in drawing clientèle from all over the 'hood as well as the suburbs. When Mack was done cutting, he scraped the remaining crumbs into a small pile, instructing Marlon to give those to the fiends as extras if they brought seven or more new customers.

Marlon had other plans for the heap of kibbles; they would be his slush fund for trickin' and smokin'.

"Sell all these for dimes, don't take no shorts. This is five hun," Mack said, already taking control of the operation. "Don't let nobody in! Serve everybody from the back bedroom window so nobody knows who or what you got in here with you."

Marlon wanted to ask how much he would get off the

51

sack, but was afraid. He counted on Mack's generosity instead, and held his peace until his new boss left. He hadn't counted on manning the window or waiting for customers, either. The good thing was that he was downstairs, giving Angelique time to cool. If it was that much cooling in the world.

After about an hour of waiting and thinking, he got some company. A thirty year-old smoker, Rose, had come to test his wares. She was small-chested with large hips and thighs. Her hair was cut short for easy maintenance. She was a very cute, dark-skinned woman with a sweet personality, but a hustler no doubt.

She told Marlon about her cousins visiting from Chicago, who were looking for good dope, saying that they would spend a hundred or so if the play was right. The only thing was, they were sick with the ZGP virus and couldn't come themselves.

"Look, I'm not fallin' for that shit," Marlon began. "They got to come they self if they want what I got."

"I told you, they all fucked up with that new shit. We go back way too far for me to be tryin' to play you. Just give me one so I can let 'em check it out; you know I'll be right back."

"Dig this, Rose, I'm gon' let you take this shake to 'em, but I still want my ten bones," Marlon told her, watching closely for a smile or any signs of trickery.

"Nigga, I'll bring yo' funky ten dollars, damn!"

"Don't get beside yo'self," he sparred, trying to let her know who the boss was.

After thirty minutes, Rose was back with the ten dollars, plus another hundred to spend. "I told you I would be back. You act like I want somebody tryin' to track me down over ten dollars." She handed him the folded bills.

Marlon looked at Rose and knew she was right. She wasn't so burnt out yet that she would run-off with something that small. In fact, she was one of the only fiends that still

52

maintained employment.

In an attempt to smooth things out, he said, "Yeah, you right. But, you know how it is out here, you can't trust nobody. Shit, I can't tell when somebody hit a bad spot and wanna try to play me. This stuff ain't even mine. Just make sure you spread the word." He watched Rose walk away, and wondered how many others had the virus, wanting to cop, but couldn't. At least he had made the first hundred dollars.

*   *   *

Mack headed for the 'hood. He knew it would be a few days before Marlon finished that first sack, but he wanted to go back later that night anyway, just to see how things were going.

He remembered his promise to call Ray when he got free. Checking his watch, he saw that it was still early, so he decided to give her time to call him. So what if he promised.

Riding past Sinai-Grace hospital, he noticed a large crowd. As he drove closer, he saw Fleetwood, an older hustler who used to sprinkle Mack with game when he was but a fledgling on the dope track.

He watched his old mentor help a slumped-over individual on a cane. He pulled closer for a better look. "Fleet!" Mack called.

"What's up, Mack? When you touch down? Let me get my sister back in the car, I need to talk to you."

His sister? Mack knew that Fleetwood's sister was no older than he was, but the person he was helping appeared to be an old woman.

He watched Fleetwood as he walked over to his truck. His wide grin revealed pearly-white teeth that contrasted the darkness of his skin. He still seemed to have his smooth style of dress, draping the freshest casual gear over his slim frame.

"Hey, baby, when you get back?" Fleetwood questioned.

"Just a few days now. What the fuck is going on at the

53

hospital?"

"Man, all those people got that new shit! The hospital start gettin' too crowded, so once they sign-in, they have to wait out here 'till they name is called. I told Sheila that I might as well take her back home; no sense in us just standin' 'round in all that commotion."

"That was Sheila? Damn! What the hell is wrong with her?"

"I just told you, ZGP. That shit been tearin' niggas out the frame! Since you been gone, seem like people been droppin' like flies. That shit is scary, young dog."

"I been hearin' 'bout it, but I ain't know it was like that."

"Yeah, it is. Be careful…you see you can't get much help from these cats.

"At first they was tryin' to tell everybody they had Lupus, 'till the news announced what was really goin' on."

"I don't know how much dope you gon' be able to move with everybody dyin', but it seems like its more young niggas dyin' than the fiends they was slangin' to. So you should be able to lock shit up quick if you get poppin' again."

The hairs on the back of Mack's neck stood at attention when he thought about the promiscuous life-style many hustlers maintained. Even worse, he thought of the way he started with Ray. "I just went to J.D.'s funeral. It seemed like it was still a lot of ballers around."

"Yeah, for now," Fleetwood began. "Think back to the line at the bathroom, I bet half those cats don't even know they infected yet. I'm tellin' you, man, I'm getting tired of goin' to funerals. Why don't you fall through and holla at me. I gotta get my sister home. She got a fever of a hundred, that's why we came."

Mack drove away thinking of all he had been told. Now, he wanted to get a drink, and forget all that madness. Hopefully, Ray would hurry and call.

Mack sat in his recliner at home, watching videos and

sipping cognac. Ninean was in the kitchen making a ruckus in her search for the right-sized pot. He knew that once she was done cooking and eating, it was off to the casino, where the degenerate gambler jacked-off most of her time and the loot she got for looking after things for Mack.

He wondered if she would ever settle down and have a family. With ZGP circulating now, he was starting to feel ready to start one himself. He knew he was just taking a trip to fantasy land when he thought of how mentally screwed-up most women in the cities were. Most were worse than the men when it came to monogamy and relationships.

After stuffing himself with Ninean's delicious entrees, he answered his ringing cell phone.

"What's up, Mack?" Ray's voice sounded over the line.

"Hey, what's goin' on? I was just about to call you."

"Yeah right, nigga! Look, if you don't want to be bothered, let me know."

Mack thought of her soft thighs wrapped around him. "Quit trippin'. If I didn't want to be bothered, I wouldn't have answered. My phone got caller I.D., too."

"So what you got up?" Ray asked in a sweetened tone.

"Nothin'. Why don't you tell me somethin' good."

"Well, I been thinkin' 'bout you all day and wouldn't mind chillin' with you. Why don't you tell *me* somethin' good, now."

"I'll be at your house in fifteen minutes," he said, then hung up the phone. Of course, he knew she wouldn't like getting hung up on, but figured it was cool this time since he was on his way.

She got in the truck, and again she wore a Mack-arousing fragrance. Her shapely legs extended from under her denim skirt, causing him to think of sliding his hands up her smooth inner-thighs.

Ray snapped him out of his trance when she asked of their plans for the night.

"What do you want to do?" he asked.

E. Scrill/DRUG LORDS

"Let's go see a movie."

Mack smiled at Ray's choice, knowing he was going to shoot to the drive-in where he could smoke, drink and possibly persuade her into a back seat game of "pin the tail on the Ray".

On the way, he stopped to see how Marlon was coming along.

"What's up? We poppin'!" Marlon began with childish excitement. "I already did three-fifty. A lot of people are at home sick, so they might send somebody to cop for them. The dumb bitch down the street tried to send her twelve-year-old son, but I wouldn't serve him."

"Good, 'cause we don't need that kind of fucked up heat. I'm glad to see you're usin' your head with this shit. Maybe now I'll be able to sleep better."

"Here is the money we made so far," Marlon said, handing over a clump of balled up bills.

"What the fuck is this shit?" Mack shouted, gunning the paper ball at Marlon's head. "That's sloppy rollin'! You gon' fuck up and loose shit like that. Organize the loot! Keep the ones, fives, and tens separate from the big bills." *Just when I thought this nigga was halfway there…,* Mack thought before he scowled, "Keep all the money 'till you finish the whole sack."

*   *   *

Angelique sat by her open window directly above the one Marlon passed his drugs through. She had been doing a great deal of ear hustling ever since the spot opened, finding the things taking place under her far more interesting than the program line-up she regularly watched on television. She snickered to herself every time Mack checked Marlon. She found it even funnier when the baseheads talked to him disrespectfully.

She was as close as she had ever been to that type of life-style, but definitely thought highly of Mack for putting the thing together; running to the window whenever she heard his truck pulling up, and scoping him out as he left.

She condemned Marlon for being the flunky, posting up by the window serving 'heads while his boss did whatever he wanted.

As she went to the window this time to watch Mack, she noticed Marlon's door keys on the table, so she locked the front door.

All respect for him was gone.

She stared at the muscular figure getting into the truck in the driveway, wanting to somehow get his attention to summon him up. But, those thoughts were quickly replaced by ones of jealousy as she noticed a female in the passenger seat, imprisoning his perception.

She knew he would have to come back pretty soon at the rate the dope was starting to move, so she planned to make herself known. She didn't even care, at that point, what Marlon would say, knowing he wouldn't talk too much shit being so afraid of his boss.

Ten minutes later, Angelique heard voices from the back, so she rushed to the window for more entertainment. Marlon was being propositioned by some crackhead. She was paper-cut skinny and raggedy as the Great Depression. Her voice was Cutty Shark rough.

He might as well get his dick sucked by her, 'cause he won't be gettin' nothin' up here, Angelique thought coldly. She was surprised when she heard the side door open followed by footsteps downstairs. She put her ear to the heat vent to hear better. She listened as Marlon finagled with the hag.

Angelique sprinted to the kitchen to grab a drink and was back in time to hear Marlon agree to oral sex for a dime-rock.

She then heard slurping and gobbling noises, knowing that he was now trying to choke his felatrix with his four-inch wonder. Angelique's eyes squinted with rage as she got up and began looking through her collection of nighties while sipping her drink.

E. Scrill/DRUG LORDS

She wanted to be prepared when her hero returned. He could get it. She knew it was a sleazy thing to do, but Mack did earn it. Knowing nothing serious would even come of it, she still wanted to be in his strong arms just once. She wanted to be at his disposal; whatever he needed of her, whenever he needed it, just because he was "the man".

Chapter 7

Donyale exited the freeway following the directions he wrote down to his daughter's house. He navigated his luxurious Buick through the streets of Detroit until he finally reached the house.

"Hello, Donny," Mrs. Fluellen began. "How was the ride?"

"It was ok. I didn't start getting sleepy until the end."

"Your daughter isn't here right now, but you can just make yourself at home. I prepared the spare bedroom for you."

Donyale looked around at the small replica of his own home.

It was quite clear that his ex-wife added her touches to them both. She expressed her good taste with fine oil paintings and expensive rugs.

He went upstairs to the room she had ready for him. It was plain, and made him feel like he was in a motel. He really didn't expect to stay in her home, but since she offered, he stayed to be closer to his daughter.

Looking at his watch, he wondered where she could be at that hour; it was past midnight. It never dawned on him that she stayed out so late. He knew she was grown, but he never came to think of his baby that way yet.

He stuck his head out of the room. "Does she stay out this late all the time?"

"It really isn't late for a person her age. She goes out sometimes, but not much. She's grown now, Donny, you have to realize that."

"But, don't you worry about her getting mugged or something? I always hear on the news how bad it is up here."

"Don't believe everything you hear from the news, Donny. You of all people should know that."

He thought of the all times he told her of cover-ups while working at the CDR. Many times there would be a true risk to public safety, but the media would lie to the nation until things were under control to prevent panic. "I guess you're right. Do you at least know who she's with?"

"Donny, if you don't sit down and relax... That girl can take care of herself," she assured.

Donyale began feeling silly for worrying, especially since he wasn't there most of the time. "I guess I'm just being old-fashioned. It seems like just yesterday we were taking her to day care."

"Yes, I remember those times, Donny. Now she is a woman, on a date."

"A date!" His thoughts see-sawed from her life being in danger to a highly intoxicated hoodlum pressuring her to smoke grass until she passed out, then submitting her to an impregnating gang-banging with his cronies.

"Donny...let me fix you a drink."

"I stopped." He wanted to, but thought of the rest of the medication he had to take. "How bad is your fever, Pat?"

"Nearly a hundred. I have been running off pretty bad lately, plus I get these awful migraines."

"I guess you see how easy it is to become infected. Do you ever worry about our daughter catching the virus while she is out with these different guys?"

"Yes, I worry. What can I do, lock her in her room? The best thing to do is educate her, and let her make the right decisions for herself. And it isn't a lot of guys. This is the first guy she's dated since she broke up with her high school sweetheart."

"Left her high school sweetheart in the dust with a broken heart, did she? We can tell what side of the family she takes after."

"I see you got jokes."

"I'm just being truthful. But, at least we're able to remain civil. It's a good thing for you, too, since I might just decide to help you seeing how you were nice enough to let me stay here and all."

"Oh, so if you had to sleep in a motel, I would just be screwed, huh?"

"Don't even try it. Why do you think I came all this way? I wouldn't let anything happen to you, even if you did use my heart for toilet paper," he assured, still using his every chance to rub things in. "I do still love you, Pat. I hope you know that."

Patricia Fluellen looked as if she wanted to speak, but didn't. She simply stared at Donyale as tears filled her eyes.

*   *   *

Ray's mind was ambushed by arousing thoughts of her night with Mack as they sat in the back seat of his truck watching the drive-in movie. She faked her fear of the film in order to get closer to him, to get his arm around her.

She looked at the surrounding cars, knowing that none of those people could see through Mack's tinted rear windows. The thought of having sex with everyone around, while they couldn't be seen or heard, thrilled her moist, and she hoped that sex was Mack's reason for recommending the back seat in the first place.

Buzzing from the cognac, she put her hand on his leg, rubbing it gently. His baggy shorts allowed her hand to glide

61

over the hairy surface. He seemed to be unaffected, so she unzipped his fly.

"I don't know if you ready to do that," he said.

Ray blushed at the comment and began caressing his balls. She felt like she finally was making progress when she saw his dazed expression as if he were hypnotized by her antics. She continued to look as his face, expecting a stream of drool to emerge from his mouth at any time.

She felt necessary, in control, as if she were a puppeteer pulling his strings. She never forgot the way the people at the funeral home showed him the utmost respect, giving up their money. She felt empowered with his world in her hands.

She thought about tasting him, but soon as the thought entered her head, fear chased it out. Having never performed the act before, she felt like he would look at her different if he discovered how green she really was. Before she knew it, she was being eased onto her back. She could see the result of her folly, magnificently erect.

    *   *   *

Mack placed his drink in the cup holder in the front seat while his fingers Houdinied him out of his shorts. When he slid off Ray's panties, he couldn't help but notice her neatly shaved crotch. *If she got ZGP, I'm probably already infected anyway,* he thought, allowing his raging hormones to eclipse his wisdom as he once again mounted her raw. He could feel her nails digging into his flesh, but paid it no mind; it was a small price to pay for admission to her choking tunnel. He ignored her pathetic sobs and grew a hump in his back.

    *   *   *

With her hair disheveled from the throes of passion, Ray went to the restroom. While there, she called to check in with her mother in case she decided to play house with Mack.

"Hey, honey," her mother began. "I need you to see if

your friend can stop by a store. I want you to bring me some aspirin for my headache."

"I don't think he'll have a problem with it. We should be leaving the movies soon."

"Why don't you just bring him with you? I would like to meet him."

Ray thought of the age gap between her and Mack. She never dated anyone as old as him before, and didn't know how her mother would respond, but would soon find out.

"My mother wants to meet you," she told Mack. The thought crossed her mind that he might feel some sort of obligation or pressure from the meeting, and just say the hell with her.

"This late?" he asked.

"She wants me to bring her something from the store, so she said to ask if you would come in to meet her. You don't have to if you don't want to."

"I realize that. I don't see a problem with just meetin' her, long as you think it'll be cool. Don't have me in a situation where I'm bein' asked fifty questions; you know I'm high."

"She cool. I think she might like you."

"I'll bet that's a big might, ain't it?"

"Only one way to find out. I might have to watch her around you, though."

After a few minutes of silence, Ray asked, "Why you bein' so quiet?"

"Just thinking."

"About what, getting rid of me now?"

"I ain't say that. You cool."

"So...are we still chillin' after you meet my mother?"

"You gon' get pregnant you keep hangin' with me."

Ray looked at him, and then looked away. She had worried before about getting knocked-up, that was her reason for making Damon wear rubbers. She never worried with Mack. The thought of him putting one in her just didn't bother

her at all.

*   *   *

    Mack pulled into the driveway where Ray lived, wondering how things would go with her mother. He hoped she wouldn't be the inquiring type.

    Ray froze and made a peculiar face, as if trying to hold in a fart. "Look, if she asks, just tell her you're twenty-six or something."

    "Awww shit! Now it's comin' out. She about to trip on me, ain't she?"

    "Naw. I just never brought nobody home except my ex, and he my age. I wouldn't bring you in if I thought she would trip on you. She might say somethin' to me later, though," Ray answered with a smile.

    Mack looked at Ray's dimple-enhanced smile. He wasn't ready to drop her off yet, felt like he could go for another shot of that ass. But, it wasn't just that, he liked being around her. She seemed so different than the other chicks in the 'hood; even had him thinking about the tether of marital bliss. Mack knew she was rare as lobster in a soup kitchen. He was almost scared to let her know how much he was diggin' her; felt like she might flip the script and try to gold-dig.

    Ray seemed to have a serious thing for him, too. He knew that his fear was probably just paranoia from dealing with so many bootmouth broads in the 'hood that were always looking for the ladder, but he didn't want to take any chances. Whatever he was going to do, he had to act fast; he just couldn't imagine a hard-core playa like himself falling in love.

    Mack told Ray, "Let me know if your mother roasts me when I leave."

    Ray forfeited her smile. "I thought I was going with you?" Her eyebrows bunched together and lips pouted.

    "Oh yeah, I almost forgot."

E. Scrill/DRUG LORDS

He got a punch in the arm for "playin' games".

Inside, Mack glanced around at the neat home, noticing the expensive things that decorated it. He didn't feel like he was in the 'hood anymore. *Damn, they got bread.*

Mack followed Ray through the kitchen, then she paused as soon as she stepped into the living room.

"Hey, baby," he heard a male voice say.

"Daddy, when did you get in town?" Ray said, smiling as she rushed out of Mack's sight with her arms outstretched. "I want you to meet my friend, Mackenzie."

Mack was glad she remembered not to introduce him by his sack name. He really hadn't anticipated meeting her father from out of town; her mother he was ready for, but this was a bit much, especially with him being high.

Chapter 8

"C'mon, quit bullshittin'," Marlon yelled through the door.

Angelique had already gone back to her bed, leaving him stranded on the stairway after hiding his keys. She never told him about the things she had heard so that he wouldn't change the things he was doing, allowing her entertainment to persist. She did tell him, however, that he would have to cuddle-up downstairs where he did his business, that she didn't want to be bothered with him that night; leading him to believe that she was unhappy with his drug dealing.

Angelique watched him cut across the backyard, through the alley, onto Davison Avenue. He then disappeared into the seafood joint.

Ten minutes later, she watched his slim figure prancing through the yard with bags. Angelique already knew his plan, but like the female mantis, she had a belly-filling scheme of her own.

*   *   *

"Where's yo' boy?" the cashier asked Marlon, referring to Mack.

66

"He should be through any time now. Do you want me to tell him you're lookin' for him?"

"Could you, please?" she answered in a sweet voice, showing him respect for the first time. "Make sure you tell him that, Faye gets off work at eleven and won't be back until six tomorrow."

"Yeah, that's my dog. I'll tell him, he's at my house everyday."

"Okay, you want somethin'?" she interjected, seeming to become irritated fast by Marlon's idle chatter.

"For free?"

"Look, you better hurry up before my boss get back."

"Cool, cool! Let me get two shrimp dinners and two--"

"I'll give you one, you got to buy the other one."

"Okay, that's cool, too. Let me get two Cokes with them." Marlon gave her some wrinkled bills from his pocket, noticing her expertly manicured fingernails, decorated with rhinestones and images of playing cards. He had been meaning to treat his woman to the nail salon, but those ideas soon ended with the loss of his job.

He watched the girl preparing his order and stared for a moment at her perfectly round behind, neatly tucked away in her tight jeans. He also noticed that her hair was professionally done, feathered, long at the top, melting into a neat taper. He figured even with her wandering eye, someone must be taking good care of her, doubting that she could afford to be so high-maintenance just frying fish.

"Here you go, don't forget to tell him. And next time, don't be lookin' at my ass." Marlon blushed at the comment, leaving, hoping to get on Angelique's good side.

"Angie, I got a little surprise for you," he sing-songed outside the door of the flat.

"What is it?" she said, playing the role.

"You gotta let me in to find out."

"It better be good. And before you come in, I hope you know it's that time of the month," she deceived.

E. Scrill/DRUG LORDS

Marlon did his best to gain stripes with her between mouthfuls of seafood promising her things to come when he got his money right; offering a massage after they ate, even offering to rub her feet.

Hearing a knock at the window downstairs, he knew he wouldn't get back in after he left. "Damn, girl, you gon' bleed to death! You can't really be bleedin', you was just on two weeks ago," he gripped, moping his way down the stairs.

Downstairs, he found the round-cheeked Rose, needing six stones, wondering at what point she would get her frequent buyer deal.

"I'll hook you up next time for real, he lied, knowing the rocks for instances such as those had been puffed to extinction.

"You better, nigga! I can always go back to where I was goin' before y'all opened."

"I got you. Now, let me take care of my other customers," he said, motioning to the figure riding a bike through the vacant lot.

"Can I get a bump 'til Tuesday? You know I'll pay you, Marlon." asked the hooded basehead through his last three teeth.

"I can't, this shit ain't mine."

"Well, smoke one wit' tha po' one. I let you smoke wit' me that time you was fienin'"

"Shh! Quit bein' so damn loud! You gon' scare the fish." Marlon tried to add humor to his words, but was really agitated now, motioning for the snaggle-tooth man to come to the side door. Knowing that if he left him out there, he would just continue his begging, eventually tipping Angelique to the fact that he blew stones with him before.

He and Marlon sat in the bedroom on milk crates, smoking a rock Marlon purchased himself. The man, giving off a foul odor of musk and gin, produced a small bumpy-faced bottle of Seagram's and passed it to Marlon. The two sat quietly waiting for more customers to come, smoking and drinking in the room illuminated only by a nightlight.

Marlon took a swig of the gin. "Why do they call you , Count Basie, anyway?"

"Fool, 'cause I likes to blow tha horn!" He waited for Marlon's smile before adding, "Fill this here trumpet with another rock, and I'll play you a song."

After Marlon served a few more customers, things were quiet again before he finally dropped some shake into his friend's stem and flicked flame to the instrument.

The Count was so happy to see Marlon coming off more dope the he performed one of his original songs. "When you check your stash, and someone has smoked all of your shit; you've been yay-young hit!"

Once the small amount of dope was gone, so was the Count, leaving only his rank smell behind.

        *   *   *

Pat Fluellen told the others to excuse her as she sprang for the stairs. Feeling her stomach beginning to churn, she knew she had better make it to the bathroom immediately. Lately, holding her bowels had become a tight fight.

She was amazed to see how much her daughter's new friend resembled her ex-husband in his younger days. She asked about his family, thinking that the two may have been related in some way. Now, she wondered if that was Ray's reason for dating him. He was older than her and didn't seem to talk much, at least not around them. She knew Donyale would have something to say about the guy, especially with him being older than their daughter. She herself wondered if Ray was ready to be involved with a man his age. That made her think back to when she was Ray's age, just meeting Donyale.

She was the more progressive of the two, both mentally and sexually. Pat had Donyale sprung from the moment they met. She believed that someone in every relationship would be on the "under", and didn't like the thought of it being her

69

E. Scrill/DRUG LORDS

daughter.

*   *   *

Donyale smiled as he watched Pat running for the stairs. He knew just what was wrong. He had told her that he would help, but said it wouldn't be for another week, that he needed to gather some supplies. He figured he would just stall a bit in order to watch her suffer. He himself was feeling better every since he had taken the capsules, so he knew they were working.

Single-handed, he had pioneered a new chapter in medical history. His only problem was how he could help others. Knowing the government didn't want the cure in the mainstream, he would have to come up with a marketing strategy to help those who wouldn't be able to otherwise receive help. He needed some form of underground peddling, but knew nothing about the streets or how they worked.

The man who makes such a discovery should be granted a Nobel Prize. But, he knew after years of working for the CDR, that ZGP was just a part of a major conspiracy; a form of population control. He may even be killed if he made it public that he had solved the virulent riddle.

He decided to worry about those matters later, only helping those that he could trust that were closest to him. But first, he would discuss the matter of Ray's new boyfriend with Pat.

Chapter 9

Mack and Ray arrived at Mack's house while the groggy sun was just starting to wake. Both were full from a breakfast at Coney Island. The cool morning air chilled them both as they left the truck and entered his home. Mack saw that his sister wasn't home yet, which was unusual. By now, she would have either lost it all, or left the casino with her winnings. He didn't think much of it, though; it gave him a chance at more private time with Ray.

"Now that wasn't so bad, was it?" Ray asked.

"Naw. Your people are cool I just didn't know what to expect. Your old man was lookin' at me kind of funny when I told him I was twenty-six. I thought he was gon' ask me for I.D. or somethin'."

"I'm surprised he didn't. He's real overprotective. He don't even think I should stay out past eleven."

"Damn, no wonder he was lookin' all crazy when you said you was comin' to my crib with me. Don't get me shot!"

"Nigga, please. My daddy ain't the type to carry guns."

"That's even worse, that mean he'll pay a nigga to do his dirt for him."

71

"Ha ha, very funny. He's a biochemist, he don't get down like that."

"Too bad he ain't got no cure for that new shit goin' around. We could get paid if he did."

"Yeah, too bad. I should have brought something to sleep in."

"For what?"

"Oh, I guess you would like it if I was naked, huh?"

"Well, that's cool with me," he said with a wide grin. "But, I do got somethin' you can wear if it'll make you feel more comfortable." He threw her his old high school tee-shirt. His dick ballooned when he saw how sexy she was in his over-sized shirt. Her smooth legs extended from under it, while her eager nipples pointed out toward him. Needless to say, she wasn't wearing the shirt very long.

Mack stirred and looked at the clock. He wanted to stay in bed next to Ray's soft body all day, but he had runs to make. He dressed, leaving Ray asleep, thinking maybe he would let her stay there with Ninean since she was home during that part of the day anyway. Even if she wasn't, he doubted that Ray would be a problem there alone until he got back. *It would be more convenient for both of us if she just stayed, she'll only be callin' in a few more hours for me to pick her up again anyway.*

He grabbed another chunk of dope from his stash, then got into his truck headed for Marlon's. Mack left his truck on the street and began walking up the driveway when he was hit by something. He looked up to see Angelique motioning for him to come up. He thought that maybe Marlon was up there, so he bypassed the first-floor flat.

Upstairs, Angelique opened the door. Her perfume mingled with the odor of rum. She wore a bathrobe and a nervous grin. "Hey, Mack. Come in, don't be a stranger now!"

"How you doin'?" he asked, noticing her untied bathrobe which was being held together by her hand. "What's up?"

"Oh, I was wondering if you could give me a ride to the store while you were here. If you're not too busy," she stated, dropping the TV remote. She bent over to pick it up, but when she stood again, her robe was wide open, bearing her luscious, naked body.

Short and strapped-the-fuck-up, huh? His erotic hunger had already been nourished by Ray, but his gluttonous sexual appetite yearned for more when he saw the tempting offering. "Oh yeah?" he questioned, referring to her making no attempts to cover herself, completely forgetting about the store.

"Yeah, I'm wide open. What you gon' do about it?" She stared expectantly into his eyes as if she wanted him to answer with actions instead of words.

He palmed one of her tits, moving closer to grip her ass.

He let go. "Damn, I wish I could, but you're Marlon's woman. I normally wouldn't care, but this is bad for business."

"I ain't his woman no more, and really haven't been for a while now. We just stay here together. He don't get none of this no more. You the one that saved me."

"You out cold! How we gon' get down with him right downstairs?"

"No he ain't. He ran out of dope, so he went to see how his mother was doing."

Mack was glad he had brought the chunk of dope. This part of delivering his drugs was unexpected, though. "That nigga love you and you know it. I can't play him like that, not with him being my worker."

Without another word, Angelique knelt before him infiltrating his fly, seizing his shaft in her small hands, opening her mouth to taste him.

Mack knew he shouldn't allow what was happening to take place, but the flesh is weak. He loved the feel of her soft, warm hands. He felt her hot breath as her mouth covered him. *Aw hell naw!* He snapped back to his senses remembering the new viral scare, and pulled back before her tongue or lips could touch him.

Leading her to the couch, he retrieved a "just in case" condom from his back pocket. He bent her over, rolling on the rubber as she positioned her elbows on the couch pillows.

"Not too rough; I haven't had sex in a few months," she said while arching her back.

"I got you." Had her he did, taking it upon himself to punish her for her infidelities; gripping her hips, pulling them to him as he plunged deep into her. A slapping sound echoed through the flat.

"It's yours, take it," she yelled.

"Not so loud, we don't want your neighbors to hear."

"Fuck them! It's all yours, now!"

After a quick shower, Angelique took her time drying Mack. "I know you got a woman, but anytime you want me, I'm here for you. Whatever you need."

"This is a one-time thing. I ain't gon' be doin' this shit in that nigga's house."

"Man, I don't even let him in no more. He left his keys, so I locked his worthless ass out."

"You bullshittin'? You don't even let him in his own house?"

"Mack, if I had somewhere else to go, I'd be gone. I don't fuck around with him anymore at all. He was downstairs screwin' one of them crackhead bitches the other night. He don't even realize I can hear everything up here."

"Oh, so this was for revenge?"

"Nope. I told you, I haven't slept with him in two months. That was just nasty what he did with her, that's all."

"You can't just keep him out of this crib like that. Y'all need to come to some kind of agreement."

"Why don't you just get rid of him? I'll sell the dope and give you all the pussy you can fuck. It ain't nothin' but

E. Scrill/DRUG LORDS

gettin' the money, then handin' the stuff out the window, right? I already heard you tell him to keep everybody out, which he don't do, and keep the lights off so nobody knows who or what's inside."

*   *   *

Weasel failed miserably at trying to talk Ninean out of her silence as he drove her to her car. He noticed that her cheek was starting to swell, where Jay had hit her no doubt. "Damn, I didn't notice your face was swollen. Did he hit you?"

Ninean looked at him, and then turned away still maintaining her silence.

He knew she wouldn't be able to keep the secret if she wanted to, not with the puffy face. "Ninean, I hope you believe me, I really didn't want anything to happen to you."

"What? Y'all just wanted to run a train on me 'cause I was drunk? Oh, yeah, I believe you didn't want him to hit me, just fuck me, that's all. It's cool. Y'all gon' get whatcha got comin'."

Weasel wasn't worried about her getting anyone, just as long as it wasn't the law. He felt like he was bad enough to deal with anyone she could get, but still didn't like the thought of being accused when he had no knowledge of the incident. "I'm the one that should be mad, that nigga stole three thousand from me, then raped my new friend, who I was planning on makin' my new woman," he said in a cheap attempt to fill her head with more of his smooth talk. It was far too late for that now; she had been violated.

*   *   *

Ninean walked into her house, and went straight to the mirror over the mantle. Seeing her inflating cheek, she began to think of her old friend, Melissa, and the way the two young punks played her while cutting class.

She had been drinking with Chuck and his friend.

75

E. Scrill/DRUG LORDS

Being involved with Chuck, they had sex, but when he went to the bathroom to wash up, he sent his friend in with her, pretending to be him, wanting more sex.

Ninean's blood boiled at the thought of the teenage game she had fallen for. No one ever seemed to take a real interest in her, only gassing her up enough to get a drunk fuck out of her. That frustrated her out of the dating scene. Then, after more than two months of a barren sex life, she was happy to meet someone, but got played like a blind hooker in a trailer park.

She began to cry out loud, releasing the anger and frustration that had been swelling up inside her. "Them punk muthafuckas! I hope Mack kill they asses!"

Frightened, she jerked as if she were having a seizure when she saw a female's reflection in the mirror, coming down the stairs behind her.

"Are you all right?" the female asked. "What happened to your face? Did you get in a fight."

"Naw, I'm cool. Where's Mack?"

"I don't know. When I woke up, he was gone."

"He left you here by yourself?" Ninean questioned in disbelief, never knowing her brother to trust a female as far as he could throw her, let alone leave one in his crib by herself. She knew right then that Mack must finally be changing, that he must really like this girl.

"I guess so."

"Y'all must really be thick."

The young woman smirked as sneaky as the cat caught with the pet canary in its mouth. "Yeah, I guess we pretty tight," she said modestly. "You better put some ice on that before it gets bigger. I know I don't know you, but if you want to talk, we can. I'm Ray."

Ninean turned to the mirror, looking at her injured cheek which was turning beet-red. "I'm cool, it's just some punk-ass nigga, that's all."

"A man hit you?"

E. Scrill/DRUG LORDS

"I got raped!" Ninean vented, heaving like a child as she cried.

Ray wrapped her with an arm of understanding, guiding her to the couch, where for an hour, she counseled and anesthetized Ninean's pain as if she were a specialist trained to do so.

Ray stopped talking to answer her cell phone.

Ninean felt as if she had known Ray for some time now. She couldn't believe that this was a girl that her brother was seeing. To her, Ray seemed intelligent, maybe even a good girl, unlike the trampy sluts she often saw Mack with. She just hoped Mack would keep her around and treat her right.

"Where's daddy," Ray said into her cell phone. "Can't he take you to the doctor?"

Ninean's ears went bionic when she heard the concern in Ray's voice.

"I'll catch a cab, then. Get ready," Ray said.

"I can give you a ride where you need to go; my car is right outside," Ninean said after watching Ray shut off her phone. She grasped the opportunity to lend a helping hand, feeling a bond between her and Ray.

Without another word, the two were on their way.

"My mother might be in emergency for a while, the hospitals have all been crowded lately," Ray said.

"Don't worry about it, girl."

Once they arrived at the hospital, they were filled with disappointment seeing that they couldn't even wait inside. Some of the ZGP zombies informed them of the overcrowding. They also told them that the hospital was being flooded with hundreds of cases, all having the same symptoms as Ray's mom.

"It might be a good idea to just go back home and wait for your father," Pat said. "He said he had something that might be able to help me."

77

Chapter 10

"Why didn't you tell me you had ZGP," Ray asked with tears streaming down her face.

"I didn't want you to worry," Pat began. "Didn't want you to be the way you are now; there's nothing you can do for me."

"Ninean began to feel sorry for Ray. She knew at least six others who had lost loved ones to the deadly virus.

"I could have been there for you more," Ray sobbed.

"You're talking like I'm dead already," Pat said.

Ninean felt as if she were dead before the words fell from her mouth. She couldn't think of anyone who survived over six months with the disorder. The only sound that could be heard in the car was Ray's sniffles. Ninean wished she had Ray's power to soothe the mind. She didn't know what to do.

*   *   *

Just as they pulled into the driveway, Pat's sphincter muscles failed her, allowing her bowels to spill into her panties. She leaped from the car as it stopped, trying to reach the house before the younger women could smell the stench, but a soon as her feet hit the ground, dizziness enveloped her;

clusters of spots and stars pulsated and exploded before her eyes; her legs turned to jelly, no longer able to sustain her weight. Pat crashed face-first into the pavement, and chipped her front tooth.

*   *   *

Ninean ignored the fecal smell, rushing with Ray to collect Pat from the driveway. Both having an arm around her neck, they dragged her five-foot-six body into the house. Ninean forgot all about her own problems as they struggled to get Pat into the bathroom so Ray could clean her before taking her to the bed. Ninean sprayed air freshener to mask the foul odor that filled the home. She ran up the stairs when Ray called, to help get Pat into bed.

"I'm going to call daddy," Ray said, looking at the caller I.D. "I found his number."

"Don't bother him, let him enjoy himself," Pat said. "He'll come back whenever he gets done with whatever he's doing."

"I'm going to call my brother," Ninean told Ray.

"No. Don't bother him with my problems."

"Girl, he must care about you. You need him right now." Ninean ignored Ray, dialing the number anyway, hoping that Mack would be able to comfort her new friend since she couldn't herself.

*   *   *

Mack skillfully chipped away at the chunk of crack with a safety pin, making dozens of ten dollar rocks. Angelique sat close by, naked, observing.

"Mack, you need to get to your girl's house, now!" Ninean exclaimed through the cell phone.

"My girl, who?" he asked, thinking that Ray was still at his crib; definitely not thinking that his sister would be at Ray's house with her.

"Your woman, nigga! Ray!" Ninean said.

79

E. Scrill/DRUG LORDS

Mack stashed the dope in the lower flat and bolted to Ray's house. He arrived at the same time as Donyale. Neither spoke a word, only exchanging nods as they waited to be let in.

*　　　　*　　　　*

Donyale stepped into the bathroom, trying to decide whether or not he was going to help Pat. He stared at his reflection in the mirror, still wondering why he had to feel so guilty for allowing her to suffer a little longer. After the way she betrayed him, he had serious thoughts of not helping her at all, just watching her die.

As Donyale entered Pat's room, he knew that her high fever had her hallucinating since she was speaking to Ray's boyfriend as though he were him.

"Donny," Pat began. "I've been waiting for you to get home from work. I need for you to check on Ray, she's sleeping in her room. I'm not feeling well."

Mack looked bewildered. He had no idea of how to respond to her.

"Ma, that's not daddy," Ray said. Her eyes once again being flooded with tears.

"Pat, I'm here, baby," Donyale said, pushing past Mack.

Pat stared at her ex-husband blankly. He knew that she was sinking deeper into her delirium; that she didn't seem to understand what was going on.

Donyale knelt beside her and caressed her face. He began to feel sorry for her, thinking how much his daughter was starting to look just like her. After the others cleared the room giving him a chance to be alone with her, he gave her the first dose of the antibiotics.

He held her face within his large palms, gazing into her eyes.

"Donny, I love you," she said. "See about my baby now, I'll be here when you get back."

80

E. Scrill/DRUG LORDS

Tears filled Donyale's eyes. He bobbled in the love they had shared, the way they had cared for one another.

He left Pat, going into the living room where Ray and her friends were.

"Why did your mother think I was your father?" Mack asked Ray.

"I told you, y'all favor," she said.

"Look, you don't have to tell me if you don't want, but do your mother got ZGP?" Mack asked Ray.

"Ray!" Donyale said, trying to keep the truth cloaked. He knew she would soon be better, and if they knew what was wrong with her, it would only tip them to the fact that he had the cure.

"Yes, she does," Ray began. "Your sister knows anyway, so it's not like you won't find out." Ray headed toward her father's voice.

Donyale couldn't believe his ears. He was too late. Now they would know the secret. He would somehow have to find a way to get them to keep quiet.

*   *   *

Mack watched Ray's graceful strut as she left the room, then turned to his sister. "How did y'all--what the fuck happened to you?" he asked through barred teeth, just noticing her bruised face.

"I met this guy last night, and we went to a motel. After we did it, he left and his friend came in..."

"So, they tried to run a train on you?" He was trying desperately to suppress his anger.

"They did!"

The answer shocked him so much he flinched. "Man, where these niggas at?" He tried not to raise his voice. "What was they names?"

"The one I met was Weasel. I can't remember his friend's name."

"Jay!"

81

E. Scrill/DRUG LORDS

"Yeah. You know them?"

"I know who they are. Look, you didn't tell the police or nobody, did you?"

"Just Ray."

"Cool. I'll take care of it, don't even worry. Which one hit you?"

"The friend."

"Okay, these niggas done went way too far." As Mack sat, torrents of homicidal thoughts drowned his mind.

*   *   *

"Make sure Pat has one of these capsules three times a day, preferably with food," Donyale began. "These antibiotics should take care of her," he told Ray, handing her a small plastic baggy filled with the medicine.

"How did you--"

"Look! Make sure you don't tell anyone about this. I don't want anyone to know that I have found a way to combat this virus. It's bad enough your friends know about Pat's condition."

"You don't have to worry about them, I think they can keep a secret."

"Good. I don't know exactly what I'm going to do yet. I'm scared to go public with it; if it was something the Government cooked-up, they'll have me killed." Donyale put his hands in his pockets and leaned his butt against the sink.

"But, daddy, you can help so many people. Why don't you sell them yourself."

Donyale looked to the floor. He wished he could do just as she said, but didn't know where to start. "It's too risky for me. I might've been able to if I had kept in contact with the riff-raffs I used to run with in my teenage years, but we lost contact after high school. Then, there's no telling who I'll be dealing with over the internet."

"How long will you be in town?"

"I'm not really sure yet. I might stay a few more days

82

to make sure that this stuff works for Pat. I don't even know what the side effects are yet. I was in such a rush to cure myself--"

"You had it, too?" Ray asked with raised eyebrows.

"Yeah, I'm afraid so. I'm doing much better. The woman I contracted it from is improving, too, so I'm hoping that Pat improves soon."

"You said something about side effects?"

"Oh yeah. My tongue always gets numb for a while after I take the stuff. So far I haven't noticed anything else, but I hope it doesn't cause any sexual problems."

"You'll be all right. You need to slow down anyway, that's how you got it in the first place. I didn't even know you had a new woman," Ray said, her words dripping with sarcasm.

"I'm not that old! We need to be talking about you and your new squeeze."

"He's fine, but do you think I can have a few of those pills for my friend, Stacey?"

"She's infected? You young people had better start protecting yourselves." He spoke hypocritically, but was trying to get the point across to Ray.

"I always protect myself, but I can't make her."

"That's the girl you went to school with, right?" Donyale asked, wondering how long Ray had been sexually active, but happy to hear that at least she did use protection.

"Yeah," Ray began. "She has been sick lately, and I don't want her to die, daddy." Ray was reaching into her trick-bag, using the tactics of a spoiled, only child like she had so many times in the past.

"It will take more than just a few pills, Ray. She would need to take three a day for at least a month. Any other drugs would lessen the effect, so none of that weed I know you guys smoke."

"Please! You know I don't be messin' around."

"That's good. I might be able to help her; let me see

how many capsules I have left."

 *   *   *

Mack sat thinking of the news his sister had just told him about Ray's father being able to help her mother. He wondered what they were in the kitchen talking about. He wished he was a fly on the wall.

Ray entered the living room smiling as if she had been granted three wishes.

"So, what did he say?" Ninean cracked after Donyale went upstairs.

"Nothin'. I'm just happy to see my parents getting along, that's all."

Mack knew she was withholding info, but didn't want to use his charm to pick her brains in front of his sister. He would wait, like had had been doing, allowing her to come to him. If he got horny before she did, he would just have to use his new plaything until she came around.

"Let me get something for your face," Ray told Ninean before going into the kitchen. She came back with half a potato. "Put this on your face. It'll hurt, but press down on the swelling. The starch will absorb the puffiness."

"A potato?" Ninean questioned.

"Yeah, it works."

Ninean did as she was told, looking at her brother as if she expected him to comment.

"How do you know about that?" Mack asked. "I couldn't picture you getting into a fight."

"My father told me."

"Is he some kind of doctor or something?" Ninean asked.

"A biochemist, but I guess he had to take all kinds of medical classes, too."

"So, he really is helping your mother, then?" Ninean questioned.

"I don't know what they're doing." Ray said turning to

E. Scrill/DRUG LORDS

Mack.

Mack couldn't wait to get Ray alone for a light-weight interrogation. "Well, since I see you're feeling better, I guess we better dip."

Ray walked over, wrapped her arms around Mack, and squeezed his butt. "Thanks for comin' to check on me," she said, her eyes twinkling as she looked into his.

"You know I'm gon' make sure you're okay. Who else am I gonna chill with if something happen to you?" he asked, planting a kiss on her lips.

"Are we gonna chill tonight?"

"Call me."

"Okay. I have to take care of my mother first, though."

Mack caught the comment, but didn't say a thing. *How would she be taking care of her mother unless she had medication?*

*   *   *

The sun's brilliant rays had Mack's leather seats scalding hot. He searched the rear of his truck for the towel on which he sat on days like that. He headed for Marlon's to see if he had received his instructions. Mack felt guilty having to face Marlon after bonin' Angelique, but figured if he hadn't someone else would've. She definitely didn't want to see Marlon anymore.

Marlon answered the door with a goofy grin.

"What the hell is wrong with you?" Mack asked, wondering how he could even smile being locked out of his own home.

"I got a surprise for you, dog."

"What? You done with that other sack already?"

"Naw, but your girl is here," Marlon said, leading Mack to the front room where Faye patiently sat.

Designer shades curtained her wandering eye, and her hair was laid as usual. Faye displayed a neon smile when she saw Mack. "Hey, Mack."

E. Scrill/DRUG LORDS

I knew this nigga was slow, but he like a breath away from havin' cerebral palsy. "Man," Mack began in an aggravated tone, completely ignoring Faye. "I thought I told you not to let nobody in here?"

"I know you know her, though."

"So! *You* don't know her, or whether she cool or not. Shit, she could have yo' ass in here tied up by now. I said nobody!"

"It was my fault, Mack," Faye cut-in. "I was tryin' to get in touch with you, that's all."

"Well, what's up?"

"You seemed pissed now, maybe I should wait 'till another time."

"I'm cool, just tryin' to get this shit goin' right. My truck is open, wait out there. I need to kick it with ol' boy for a minute" Mack said, keeping in mind that Angelique had ears like satellite dishes.

Faye's back pockets swung like twin pendulums as she switched her way out the door. The strong sent of Glow by JLO lingered after she left.

Mack turned disappointed eyes to Marlon. "Man, don't do that shit no more! That's the best way to set a nigga up; wit' a bitch! Did Angelique give you the rocks?"

"Yeah, but she still trippin' on me. I'm gettin' sick of her ass."

"You need to sit down and talk to her."

"She got me locked out the crib." Marlon's face displayed humiliation as he looked down at his badly scuffed gym shoes.

"Out of your own crib?"

"Yeah," Marlon exhaled.

"Well, that's y'all," Mack began. "Fuck it! Just stay down here and roll. She'll come around when she see how fat yo' pockets get." Mack knew that his words would motivate Marlon to keep doing his bidding.

"Yup! She gon' catch the vapors if she keep actin' like

that."

"Don't speak it, live it!"

In the truck, Faye had nothing to say except that she was no longer with her man.

"For real?" Mack said, not really surprised. He knew she had a crush on him when he used to knock-off her friend, Brandy. He just had no interest in Faye back then being the skinny, cock-eyed girl she was. He knew that if she was going through all this trouble to alert him of her availability, she would definitely be willing to give her all for the purpose of being in his circle, even if she wasn't his significant other.

At least now, she had filled out considerably, having an hourglass shape, but still the dancing eye.

"Yeah, I told you I would give you a holla if my situation changed. So, what's up?"

Mack knew that his plate was full enough, but didn't want to turn her down without giving her a test drive. "I'm not really lookin' for a woman right now. I got too much other shit goin' on to tie myself down like that. Shit, I just got out the joint."

"Nigga, I know I can't tie you down. But, we can still be friends."

Mack looked over at her, happy to see that she got the point. He gave her his number, promising that they would hook-up later. He watched her big butt as she got out of the SUV. He would get to her soon enough, but first, he had to find out what secrets Ray had about the new virus.

If it was a cure that she knew about, he would have to get his hands on it, then there would be no more poison-pushin'. He wanted to make a change anyway, but if her father had the cure for ZGP, it would be time to get some real dough; legal dough.

Mack's cellphone vibrated on the dashboard.

"Mack," Stan's voice sounded through the phone. "I need you to meet me."

"What's up?"

E. Scrill/DRUG LORDS

"I'll tell you when I see you. You know where."

Mack raced to the spot where he met Stan before, lowering the truck's visor to block the rays of the setting sun.

Mack sat up front while Stan's younger cousin sat in back.

"What up, big fella?" Mack said.

"Some niggas robbed Noah at my weed spot," Stan said.

"What? When you start sellin' weed?"

"Shit, my oldest son's uncle got a green thumb. His momma kicked him out, so I set him up in one of my cribs. Told him all he had to do was watch the weed he grow for me in the backyard."

"So that's where you get all that good shit from?"

"Yeah. Noah, tell him what went down."

"This dude that used to steal gym shoes from people at my school back in the day came in when I was servin' a customer, actin' like he was robbin' both of us, but the other dude ran out with him."

Mack nearly cracked a smile listening to the okee-doke they ran on Noah. "Do you know they names?"

"The one that came in with the gun was Weasel..."

"I know who you talkin' 'bout."

"Can you find them?" Stan asked.

"Maybe." Mack knew if Stan wanted them bad enough the price on their heads would escalate the more difficult the task was.

"If you find them both," Stan began. "I'll throw you a half-bird. If you bring them alive, you get a extra pound of this sticky-ass weed."

Mack couldn't believe what he was hearing. He was about to be paid a half-kilo to take care of the fools who raped his sister. "Cool. You know how I get down; that shit is a done deal!"

"Is that hamburger joint open?" Stan asked, holding his stomach. "I hope I don't got that new virus, man. I been havin' a fever all week, stomach been bubbly as hell! A nigga can write his own ticket if he can get rid of this shit."

A smile curved Mack's mouth as he watched Stan run to relieve himself. He couldn't wait until Ray called so he could get the scoop. Hopefully, she would hold the key to his exit from the dope game for good.

Mack thought about the task ahead of him: bringing in Weasel and Jay, dead or alive. He knew it wouldn't be too much to handle. He had done things like that so many times before, but had already made up his mind to get someone else to do it. He could still make a profit from the job.

He got into his own truck, heading for the titty-bar where his old friend, Johnny, worked the door.

Chapter 11

John Dollar stood at the entrance of Woody's , the livest titty bar on the west side, patting down each person who entered, making sure no one gained access with a weapon of mass destruction. The small bar overflowed with ballers from every part of the city, all wanting to flash gaudy bankrolls in front of the bad bitches shaking their thonged asses.

Patrons could sit at any of the tables that surrounded the stage in the center of the floor for free, but in order to get one of the booths that lined the walls, one had to tip Johnny or one of the other bouncers twenty dollars or more. The corner booths saw the most action since they had more room and provided a playa with more privacy in case he wanted to get his dick rode.

Mack parked his ride, and then entered. He and Johnny slapped palms, and then pulled each other together in a tight embrace without saying a word. When they released one another, they both smiled and slapped palms again. Mack was permitted entry without being frisked.

Johnny scratched his scalp along a part between his braids and said, "Gimme 'bout twenty minutes, dog."

Mack went to the bar and ordered a shot of tequila. He

90

E. Scrill/DRUG LORDS

banged his shot and took his time eyeballing each of the dancers casting their spells of temptation inside the small trick trap. Mack watched as Johnny motioned for him to go out to the parking lot before he escorted one of the dancers to the girl's room.

"That bitch was bad as hell, wasn't she?" Johnny asked.

"Oh yeah, I know you fuckin' at least one of them ho's in there."

"I took down a few. Somethin' I do every now and then, but I ain't tryin' to catch no feelin's for those hookers," Johnny said.

"What else been goin' on with you?" Mack queried.

"Layin' low. With all the hot shit we did before you got knocked, I needed time to cool off. I knew it was gon' be on and poppin' soon as I saw you."

"Oh, so you ready?"

"Man, come on! Ross ready, too!"

"Ross? I thought that nigga was dead."

"Everybody he thought tried to kill him is dead. He just been below the radar, fuckin' 'round with some fat bitch out in Oak Park."

Mack was at first glad to hear the mention of Ross, but remembered the last time he employed Ross and Johnny to abduct a snitch to see how much he told police about a fellow baller's drug operation.

The two had their orders, but thought that maybe they would rough him up a bit before bringing him in. After being beaten within an inch of his life, the abductee was no good for interrogations. When Mack asked why they beat him before he could be questioned, the two dangerous individuals simply offered, "Well, what you expect us to do? He was resistin'."

Mack looked at Johnny, who was just a few inches shorter than he, and said, "Look, dog, I got a mission for y'all, but don't kill these two niggas. I'll throw y'all a big eighth apiece, but if they still breathin', y'all get a extra half-p of the

91

stickies to split."

Johnny's eyes bulged as he asked, "A eighfy, plus a half bow of the Afghans--bet!" Johnny yanked his crotch a few times before saying, "Leave the yola soft, I got a few custos that like to powder they nose."

"I wasn't gon' rock that shit up for y'all anyway. Y'all niggas know how to cook; I got enough problems schoolin' this green-ass nigga sittin' in my joint on Clements."

"Damn, you don't waste no time, my nigga! Do I know him?"

"You know Marlon ho-ass."

"That nigga that used to cut the grass back in the day? Damn, he graduated to the dope game, huh?"

"If that's what you wanna call it. Got a bitch badder than li'l mama that just got off the stage." Mack tried to hold back a wide grin before adding, "She a noisy little bitch, too."

"You fuckin' her? That's cool, 'cause I know we gon' have to cross Marlon's T. The health department been tryin' to close the bar down anyway 'cause of that ZGP shit; so I need all the work I can get."

"Naw, I ain't gon fuck wit' her no more. I got a bad bitch myself."

"You got a woman?"

"I ain't say all that. She cool, though," Mack said.

"You ain't come get me to hang wit', so I know you probably been tryin' to knock the bottom outta her ass. Been hittin' it every day since you touched down, huh?"

"Pretty much," Mack exhaled.

"Now think about what Fleetwood used to tell us, 'bout ho's when we was comin' up. It don't matter what you say 'bout 'em, if you fuckin' her every day, you might as well call her yo' woman."

Trying to quickly change the topic, Mack said, "Man, just hit me up as soon as you get off."

*   *   *

E. Scrill/DRUG LORDS

Mack bounced his truck down Hubbell, wondering if he should get someone else to handle Weasel and Jay in order to bring them to Stan alive. He knew Johnny would find a reason to hurt them. Mack began to think of Johnny's sadistic ways growing up.

If Johnny got lucky and found a litter of puppies or kittens, he would have to play rocketship. He would pack six or eight of the newborns in a bucket that had a string tied around the handle. Next, he would hold the string while spinning as fast as he could. The faster he twirled, the higher the bucket would fly. Centrifugal force sucked the small, frightened animals to the floor of the spacecraft. Once Johnny got dizzy, he would yell, "Blast off," releasing the string, sending the doomed critters soaring through the air. After landing in another backyard, the yowling survivors would slowly limp away, trying to escape before Johnny could send them on another mission.

Mack's cell phone buzzed in his pocket. "What's up Ray?" he asked.

Mack stopped to kick it with his sister before going to get Ray, just to make sure that she really was okay. He knew that she could be going through some real mental trauma even if she wasn't allowing him to see it.

Mack looked at his sister as she watched videos in her room. She seemed to be just looking in the direction of the television, not really paying it much attention. He didn't really know what to say to her. For all he knew, she could be developing a hatred toward all men; this being her second time being sexually assaulted, that he knew of anyway.

"You ok, 'Nean?"

"Yeah, just thinking."

"You goin' to the casino tonight?"

"I really don't feel like it. I guess it's getting old."

"You sure? You can have some loot if you need it."

"Thanks, but I'm cool. Don't worry about me, I ain't gon' let that shit get to me like that. Thanks, Mack, for caring."

"You know I got the situation under control, Sis."
Ninean looked at Mack. With a blush, she said, "I know, big Bro."

*   *   *

Ninean felt lucky for having Mack for a brother. She was always respected in school and throughout the 'hood. She knew he would handle the situation better than the authorities could.

Her mind flashed on the time some young punks robbed her for her gym shoes. Mack scoured the 'hood until he found the culprits. He relieved one of his teeth, while the other sustained a broken jaw. She never got her shoes back, but she didn't feel as bad having Mack on the case.

She had no desire to gamble anymore, feeling that the incident with Jay wouldn't have happened if she wasn't out gambling. But now, she needed something else to do with her time. If she had a man, she would spend time with him. She decided to go see a movie; she hadn't been to one in quite some time. She knew whatever she decided to do, she wasn't going to feel any better sitting around the house.

*   *   *

Mack sat at the bar of the Olive Garden with Ray. He decided to have a few drinks while they waited for a table. He told her that he was taking her out to celebrate.

"Celebrate what?" Ray wanted to know.

"I'll tell you when the time is right," Mack assured with a wink.

After feasting on the Italian cuisine, Mack told Ray to drive.

"Where we goin' now? Are we still celebratin'?"

"Oh, we gon' be celebratin' for a while, baby." Mack watched Ray display an electric smile as she took the keys. He cupped her blue-jeaned behind and pulled her near to him.

94

E. Scrill/DRUG LORDS

The full moon twinkled in Ray's pupils as she looked up at Mack. She opened her mouth to kiss him as he lowered his head to her, but he kept past her mouth and dropped his nose to her Cool Water fragranced neck.

"Damn, you smell good," he said.

"You crazy!" she said, still blushing.

As Ray whipped the SUV down the freeway, Mack moved closer to her, still taking whiffs of her perfumed neck.

"Stop, you gon' make me crash," she told Mack, who was now under her shirt, palming her tits.

"I was gon' swing by the Fox to see what was poppin', but I think we better call it a night."

"No! I want to go. They got a old-school concert tonight. I ain't ready to go home yet," Ray said with a frown.

"I ain't say you was goin' home." Ray looked over at Mack as if she could read his mind.

Mack cycled his eyebrows and said, "That's right, baby, you know what time it is," in a sexy bedroom voice before planting a delicate kiss on her cheek. He watched her face light up as he settled back into his seat.

He knew he was starting to get to her with his sweetness, and was having a good time doing it, too. He planned to take her to the point of no return once he got her home; there he knew he would be able to get in her head and find out what was really going on.

*   *   *

Marlon heard Angelique creeping up the stairs back to the upper flat. He scampered to the door to catch her.

"Angie, let me kick it with you," he said.

He followed closely as she opened the door so he wouldn't be locked out again. He scanned the living room for his keys.

"What you do with my keys?"

"I ain't do nothin' with 'em. Where you leave 'em at?"

Marlon spent over an hour looking for the keys before

95

finding them between the couch cushions.

"Why didn't you help me find my keys?"

"I ain't loose 'em," she said in a sassy way.

"What's really up? You been actin' cold and short towards me lately; it ain't just the keys, either."

"Maybe it's PMS," she said in a stank way, then nearly cracked a smile as if she knew she had burnt out the time-of-the-month routine.

"I see you 'bout to smile; you know you fulla shit!"

Angelique vented a burst of laughter. "You just paranoid. That's what smokin' that shit do to you."

"So, you gon' try to use that against me?"

"I ain't usin' nothin'. Quit trippin' and gimme some money."

Marlon began to feel better since she was at least asking him for something. He figured it might even lead to something good. "What you need money for?" he quizzed.

"Some pads," she said before laughing hysterically.

"I'm gone," he said, heading for the door.

She quickly straightened her face before asking, "I ain't good for no money, Marlon?"

"I ain't got it right now; this Mack's loot."

"Maybe I'll ask him for some then."

She struck a nerve. The thought of Mack pulling Angelique petrified Marlon; he knew he would never get her back then.

He looked at her, waiting for her to at least say, "Sike." But no. She just looked up at him as if he were supposed to give up Mack's cash. He had already smoked more than he should have from the sack, and was planning on telling Mack he would just work off the shortage.

"How much you need?"

"Two hundred."

Damn, I knew she was gon' say some shit like that. Just when I get this bitch doin' a gee a day, I go fuck up this nigga's dough. I only get thirty off a hundred, and I smoked

96

'bout ten stones today already. *This bitch gon' have to give up*
some pussy 'cause I know Mack gon' fuck me up if I give her
that loot. "You askin' for two hun and won't gimme no ass?"

"Marlon, I'm supposed to go shopping with Fat Trish.
They on they way to get me now. Just have your rubber ready
when I get back…okay? Gimme the money so they don't
leave me."

Marlon began to cheese at the mention of him actually
getting his bone-on, but after thinking, he said, "Damn, I got to
wear rubbers now, too?"

"I forgot to take my pill the last couple days. You
know I ain't tryin' to get pregnant."

Mentally vanquished, Marlon peeled off two hundred
dollars. He tried at first to give her all ones and fives, but she
made him surrender ten twenties.

She never even thanked him before she ran to Trish's
tooting horn.

Marlon went back downstairs to work the window. As
soon as he got comfortable, the Count once again graced him
with his presence.

After parking his bike in the basement, the horn blower
peacocked past Marlon in his dress slacks and white dress
shirt. The sound of his church shoes striking the kitchen floor
tiles echoed throughout the flat. He was clean-shaven with a
facial expression that said to the world, "I'm the spice!"

Count Basie took his usual corner seat on the milk
crates and said, "Marly, I know you gon' match me a few
bumps."

"Match you? You got money?"

"Hell yeah. My broad just got paid and took me out to
dinner. I guess she wanted to let me know how much she
appreciated the ol' love machine." The Count stood gyrating
his hips in a vulgar display of his sexual abilities before he
continued with, "Yeah, I may be a old dog, but I still can lay
pipe."

"Yeah, whatever," Marlon said thinking of the thrills

that were promised to him.

The Count wasted no time in whipping out his gigolo-dough before saying, "I got me a new horn, and I'm ready to blow!" He reached into his shirt-pocket and pulled out a shot-sized gin bottle, custom made to smoke crack out of.

"You don't be bullshittin', do you?" Marlon knew a basehead could turn almost anything into a crack pipe when necessary. This made him think of his old Uncle Doobie.

Everyone told Marlon that his uncle was a fiend, but Marlon remained in a state of denial, until one day he noticed his television antenna getting smaller. Each day it seemed to lose a few inches. After the antenna finally disappeared, so did the television.

Marlon took a ten dollar bill from the Count, then let him choose one of the stones he had left. The Count sparked the stone and took a greedy drag from his horn. Soon the two were high as giraffe pussy, sitting in the dark quiet with eyes as big as saucers. Every five minutes Marlon would run to the window and peek out.

"Damn, man, why don't you sit down somewhere? You blowin' my high. You know ain't nobody out there," said the Count.

"I thought I heard somethin'."

"Man, you know you ain't heard nothin'. Y'all newjacks can't even control the high. I know one thang, though; you better lick them white-ass lips 'fore I spit on 'em."

Marlon darted his tongue out over his parched lips. They were so dry that it felt like his tongue would stick to them. This was a result of the air passing over them as he sucked on the pipe.

Paranoia began to set in, and Marlon began to wonder if he had dropped any of the remaining stones when he allowed the Count to pick one from his hand. He stooped down, bug-eyed, scanning the frizzy carpet for anything close to being white in color. When he had no luck after a few moments, he got on his hands and knees, flicked his lighter to combat the darkness, and continued his search for the phantom kibble.

"Man, you trippin', Marl," Count Basie began. "I might have to cut you off if you can't do no better than that. You ain't even outta dope yet, and you actin' like you done dropped a kilo."

Marlon jumped at the Count's words as if he forgot that he had company. Feeling foolish, Marlon stood and peeked out the window again.

The Count chuckled before he began with another of his originals. "Yo' bitch said she love you, that she'll put no one above you; she lied to ya, she lied to ya! On the blue moon she gave ya the ass, an' she said it was good, but you know you came too fast; she lied to ya, she lied to ya!"

Marlon quickly spun on his heels to face the Count. "What the hell you talkin' 'bout?"

"I'm just doin' me. What's the problem?"

Marlon felt like the Count's song was hittin' a little too close to home, like maybe he had heard something. *Naw, couldn't be.* "I'm just trippin', man. Gon' on, do yo' thang."

"I will not sang another line until you pull out a rock to match mine. Get-highs on you now, baby boy. Blaze-up!"

Before Marlon could pull out another stone, he got a knock at the window. It was Rose.

The Count's eyes lit up at the sound of the woman's voice. Scrambling over to the window, he said, "I got this one, Marl."

Marlon handed him two stones and sat on the crates to watch the show. He figured the Count would go deep with his game for her.

"Hello, beautiful," the Count began. "May I be of service to you?"

"Where Marlon at?" Rose wanted to know.

Basie mustered his best Pacino voice. "I has him close by." He came back to himself and continued with, "But I thank the heavens that I now have a chance to be of service to a divine enchantress such as yourself."

Marlon continued to watch as Rose sparred with, "Well, can this divine enchantress get two for fifteen?"

The Count cracked a Kool-Aid smile. "Oh, hold on, I think I hear Marlon comin' back."

Marlon served Rose, then called Basie back to the window to avoid dealing with the hag who licked him up for the dime-rock. He knew she never intended to pay full price since he tricked with her that one time. That was just one of the games the fiends would try to run if allowed to.

The Count stepped to the window and took an imperial stance. "Oh, damn. It's just you. What the hell you want?"

Marlon hoped that the Count knew her. "Aye, man, you cool with her?" he asked, hoping that Basie wasn't running off a customer.

The Count looked down at her with his ashy mouth shaped into a frown. "She cool; the pussy ain't shit, though."

The beef was on! After a few harsh remarks about the Count's baby-making tool, the hag in her rough voice asked, "Where Marlon?"

"Why?" the Count asked. "I'm holdin' thangs down."

"Well, you wanna do somethin'? I ain't got but three dollars till my check come."

The Count turned to Marlon. "It's party time!"

*   *   *

After his two week stay, Donyale made sure that Ray had the treatment of her mother understood, and headed for home to assist Melinda with the capsule making. He had stashed, underneath the dresser in Ray's bedroom, enough of the medication to cure a dozen inflicted individuals. That was his back-up batch, just in case.

He no longer had any symptoms of infection, and he knew that Melinda should be done with her doses as well.

While driving through Kentucky, he decided to call to see how much of the ingredients she had left. If necessary, he would be able to stop and get whatever was needed on his way.

Sounding like she was in good spirits, she informed him that she had whipped together enough medicine to cure a hundred people.

After driving another five hours, he finally made it home. When he walked in, there was soft music playing, and the only lights were from scented candles. When he looked down, he noticed he was standing on a trail of flower petals leading to his bedroom.

When he entered his sleeping chamber, there stood Melinda. Her hair was flawlessly done, and her lipstick matched the camisole which revealed a pubic patch trimmed into a downward arrow.

"Hey, baby," she began in an erotic tone. "I got everything ready for you. I know how you must feel about me, but if you didn't do what you did, I wouldn't even be alive. I know I can't ever repay you for that, but..." She looked to his fly before continuing. "I can't see why I should ever stop trying."

Damn, she's looking good! Donyale was tired from his ten hour hump, but he was still a man who hadn't been sexed in months. Lately, he had been thinking only of how she had burned him. He forgot about the sexual servitude she promised him before he left for saving her.

Chapter 12

Ray tried not to listen as Mack talked on his cell phone. She already realized that he was a dopeman, but wasn't going to let that small fact disrupt the happiness she felt when with him. And today he was in rare form, treating her like a princess.

She overheard him tell someone on the phone, "Slide by my spot. I need you to do somethin' for me."

Ray believed him to be heavy in the game by the way he carried himself and treated others. She knew from a few of her cousins that the hustlers who treated others respectfully lasted longer than those who acted like they were all that. She felt good about the way her Mack treated her, and knew she was more to him than just a jump-off broad. She felt comfortable sharing herself mentally with him because of the way he handled the conversations with a certain resolved wisdom.

Ray knew that Mack more than likely was ruthless in the streets or else he wouldn't be able to thrive like he seemed to. But, when he was with her, he was always tender and unselfish, making her feel as if she was in a land of passionate resonance; she therefore yearned to share more intimate moments with him.

She sat on Mack's soft bed and watched as he took off her shoes and began to massage her feet. He took the time to care for each of her toes, then kneaded her arch with the heel of his hand.

Much to Ray's dismay the doorbell rang, and Mack sprinted down the stairs without a word.

Ray tried to look down from his bedroom window to see who it was, but only saw the top of some guy's cornrowed head. She hustled back to her spot.

He returned with his shirt in his hand. This was the first time she had a good look at the chiseled physique that had been concealed by his clothing.

Damn, Boo, I knew you was buff, but I ain't know you was cut-up like that!

In a white flash, his shirt bombed her in the face. She tried to throw it back, but he ducked and grabbed her by the ankles. Ray was slowly being dragged from the bed as she looked at the devious smile on Mack's face. Her bottom slid off the bed and hit the floor. Ray struggled to free her legs while playfully shouting, "I'm gon' get yo' ass!"

Mack was unwittingly dispelling Ray's thoughts that having an older boyfriend would be boring. She didn't at all think she would have fun, playful times with him.

Oh, so you wanna play rough? I'll fix you for hittin' me with that shirt.

Now all she wanted to do was jump on his back and place his muscles, scented with Kenneth Cole's Black, under arrest--until he gave of course.

As she moved to get up, Mack put his hand on her shoulder, stopping her on her knees.

Ray, who was now eye-level with Mack's zipper, looked up at him as he said, "I know you gon' get me back, but I give for now."

She looked at his crotch before he said, "I hope you don't mind being my woman."

103

E. Scrill/DRUG LORDS

Ray looked up so fast that she nearly got whiplash. *He just want me to suck it, that's all. I guess he's worth it.* "Do you think I mind? And why you got me all on the floor--" Before she could finish her words, her neck was lassoed with a cold necklace. She lifted it by the heart-shaped charm it carried. The crystalline emblem was filled with a clear liquid that amplified the twinkles of the half-dozen diamonds that lined its bottom.

I get this fine-ass man, plus ice? Now that's what I'm talkin' 'bout! Man, gimme this dick, Ray thought as she reached to infiltrate Mack's fly.

"Hold up," he said, seizing her wrist. "It's all about you today, remember?" He pulled her to her feet. "But don't think that I don't want a rain check on that." He pressed his lips to her blushing mouth before pushing her onto the bed. Ray lifted herself to allow Mack to slide her thong and jeans over her hips. She held the heart up to the light and marveled at its congealed brilliance as she felt Mack sucking hickeys up her inner thigh. His arms slid under her legs as his hands stretched up her shirt to capture her breasts. She dropped the chain to her chest and grabbed his ears as he began lapping her honeyed core.

Oooh shit! "Oooh shit," she moaned using his ears to navigate Cupid's arrow that lashed from Mack's mouth to her most intensely sensitive points.

This was the first time for her, and she nearly cursed Damon out loud for the years she stuck with him, yet he refused to hurdle the boyish obstacles that kept him from conjuring mind-blowing moments such as these.

Damn, I ain't know this shit would feel like this! Feel sooo gooood! Don't do it like that, baby; you gon' get me hooked! she thought as she arched her back. She definitely knew she didn't want him to stop, but she was fearful of becoming sprung. She turned her head from side to side as she struggled to maintain her composure, battling the demonic forces that possessed Mack, empowering him with heartshackling dynamics. *Whoa, what the--* "Ahhh, Mack," she purred as she melted with limpness, orgasmically defeated.

After showering with Mack, Ray told him, "I gotta go home to see about my mother."

On the way to her house, they listened to the radio as the newest ZGP warning announced that the virus had reached pandemic levels throughout the country. Ray looked over and locked eyes with Mack as they continued to ride in silence.

Ray stuck her head into her bedroom to make sure that everything was in order before she let Mack in, then went to administer the antibiotic dose to her mother. With her mother sick in bed, she knew she would have privacy in her room.

Ray walked over to the chair on which Mack sat and took a seat on his lap. She leaned back in his embrace and received a peck on the cheek.

I don't know why I even got this extra medicine from my father, but since I have it, I wonder if I should trust Mack to sell it. I know he deals with people that know how to keep they mouth closed. And I know he can maybe be the hustler my father needs to carry out his plan. I just hope our relationship doesn't become based on my connection to this stuff, 'cause I know I can get more. Damn, I want to tell him, but I don't really know if I should. Ray's thoughts were interrupted when Mack asked, "So what's wrong?"

"Nothing. I was just thinking, that's all."

"Well, if you want to talk about it, I'm here."

Understanding, too? I love you, Mack. Ray reached into her bosom and produced the small baggy filled with the capsules given to her by her father for her friend, then handed them to Mack. She watched Mack's face light up and his mouth transform into a wide smile as if he already knew what the plastic baggy contained. Ray smiled also; she felt good for being able to make him so happy. She had never seen him smile like that before.

"What's this," he asked.

Nigga, you fake as hell! "You know what that is. Quit

105

playin'," Ray said, watching his eyes closely, wondering if he really knew what the capsules were.

"Tell me. What are they?"

Why is he smiling if he don't know? He just playing games. "That's okay. Give 'em back. I guess I'll have to keep 'em if you don't know what they are." Ray made a comical face to counter the bullshit she knew Mack was trying to run.

"Hold up! You gave 'em to me, now they mine! Mmmm, let me guess now…" Mack closed one eye and looked to the ceiling as if he was searching the catacombs of his mind before he continued with , "Magic beans! That's it, I'll plant 'em and grow a--"

Ray jammed a pointy elbow into his chest before saying, "You crazy. For real though, you know how I told you what my father does, right?" Without awaiting an answer, she continued with, "Well, he made a cure for that new virus, and he want it on the low-low."

"Everything I do is on the low-low."

"I know, but the thing is, he made it clear that the reason he won't go public with it is because he thinks the Government is behind ZGP, and might try to kill him if they know he got a cure." She looked him in the eyes. "I don't want to lose you 'cause of this stuff. You got to promise me you'll be careful."

Mack pulled Ray's mouth slowly to his, and for about two minutes their tongues danced a concupiscent waltz.

After Ray gave Mack a complete rundown on all of the specifics concerning the antibiotics, Mack said to her, "I don't know your father's situation and how he got this, but I know we can get paid if he can keep it comin'. How much do you think he got anyway?"

"I don't know. I guess he just makes whatever he needs."

"Straight up? That's like gettin' dope for free. Do you think you can get more?"

"Maybe. I just don't know how much more."

"Damn, he da' man! He got the game on lock, huh? Well, I appreciate the fact that you shared the secret with me."

"Mack, all kinds of good things can happen if you treat me right." *Damn, I ain't mean it like that.* "I mean, don't try to be good to me just 'cause you think I can get you more of this stuff. What I should have said is that I will do all I can to help my man."

"I been lookin' for a way to get out the dope game." He pierced Ray's soul with the heart-softening facial expression of a puppy. "I guess all this with us was meant to be. I'm glad I got you on my side, not because of this medicine, but because...I don't know, it's just somethin' in you that I need in my life. I ain't had a woman since like...high school."

"Get up for a minute," Ray said, getting up herself. Once Mack stood, Ray sat down. "Come here," she said reaching to undo his pants. As she slid his pants down, she felt his hand come to rest on her shoulder.

All kinds of good things can happen if you treat me right.

*   *   *

Angelique walked up the driveway of her flat with shopping bags in both hands. She waved to her friend as she entered the front door, then tried to once again catwalk up the steps without Marlon hearing.

Cool, he must be sleep down there, she thought as she entered the living room. As she went into the bedroom, she saw Marlon lying nude across the bed.

"What's up, baby? Finally made it back, huh?" he asked.

Fuck! I knew I should've went to get something to eat with Trish, too. Oh well, he still ain't gettin' none, she reasoned. "Hey, what's up. I see you ready."

"And you know it," he said with a wide grin.

E. Scrill/DRUG LORDS

"Let me get settled first. Dang."

She tried to take forever putting up her new clothes and undressing, but she still seemed to be moving too fast. She dreaded the very thought of him touching her. Since she no longer had any feelings for him, he just seemed so dusty, and while he needed a haircut, he looked to her like he might even stink. She could feel his binocular vision molesting her as she shucked her clothes and stood in her panties.

"I'm 'bout to get a drink. Hold up," she stalled.

Damn. Think, Angie, think! How can I get out of this? I know!

Angelique snatched the bottle of rum from the kitchen cabinet and walked back into the bedroom, sliding under the covers next to Marlon. She smiled inside, watching him with peripheral focus as he stared while she sucked away the bottle's contents. He was lit up like a bonfire, as if he just knew he was about to strike gold.

Angelique capped the bottle and began to erotically wiggle off her panties. As soon as her bush popped from under the silky drawers, Marlon reached for his rubber.

"Let me roll it on you," she said as she watched his horny eyes follow the panties to the floor.

"It's all good. Here."

She took the condom, then reached for his penis. She examined it closely, holding in her laugh as she thought about its pygmy stature while fully erect.

"What's this?" she asked, referring to a small discolored patch of his skin that she already knew was there.

"That's my birthmark. You seen that before. Quit playin'."

"Naw, I don't remember you havin' that. I ain't tryin' to catch nothin', Marlon. I want to give you the pussy, but you need to get checked out. I know you ain't been cheatin' have you?"

"Man, c'mon!"

"C'mon nothin'! You need to get checked out first. I

E. Scrill/DRUG LORDS

don't know what none of them crackhead bitches gave you, but that don't look right."

Marlon's face looked as if he had braved long Christmas Eve shopping lines with two baskets of groceries, only to find out when he got to the check-out that his food stamps were counterfeit. Angelique dropped his deflated dick in an icky way, like it was a turd.

"Marlon, you need to get checked out. I can't believe you even tried to give me some shit after you know you been fuckin' 'round out there somewhere," she protested in an ingenious offense that she knew would seal Marlon's sexual fate. "After all the shit I been through wit' yo' punk ass, you gon' cheat and let a bitch give you something? Nigga, you don't deserve none of this ass! You might as well go back to that bitch who gave you that chocolate chip dick. I ain't even sleepin' in the same bed with you. I thought we could work shit out, but naw! You had to go and get burned. Trish already told me if I need a place to sleep, I can come over her house. So if you gon' sleep in here I'll leave," she lied, getting out of bed, knowing that he wouldn't allow her to leave.

"Man, I ain't even do shit wrong. Hold up. I'll go downstairs, but I ain't cheat."

She remained quiet, faking like she had suddenly become interested in the television.

"You trippin'," Marlon said, gathering his clothes. He walked out of the room with his head down, intellectually murdered, to man the window downstairs, and perhaps regroup for a romantic comeback.

Bye-bye, little boy.

*   *   *

John Dollar walked the last dancer to her car, then went to assist with the rest of his duties that concerned closing the bar. He was anxious to get back into the streets and make some real money. His start only consisted of dropping off a package that he picked up from Mack during his lunch break, but it was a start. Since he didn't start work until six in the evening, he would have plenty of time to enforce the flow of Mack's cash--amongst other things.

He sat at the bar watching as the barkeep cleaned things up. He and a few other bouncers were given the remains from a fifth of vodka to smash while they waited to walk the rest of the employees to their cars.

Once everything was closed, he hopped into his old-school Regal and pulled off pumpin', Loose Ends, from his six-by-nines. He whipped into the gas station at the corner of McNichols and Schaeffer, and noticed the barkeep, Sonya, fueling her vehicle. He took his keys with him even though his co-worker was there.

His '84 Buick was his baby. He had his seats piped out in gray and burgundy with a single dollar sign on each head rest. The steering wheel and everything else inside was wood grain, even the knick-knacks like the top of the gear shifter which rose from the hump in the floor between the two front seats. The outside was rainy-day-gray with a multitude of navy blue metallic flakes embedded in the paint, all winking reflectively.

The harmonic growl of the chrome, dual tail-pipes announced the presence of a diabolical engine. The masterpiece was elevated by a set of chrome twinkies, wrapped with mustard and mayonnaised tires.

Johnny pushed open the service station door and noticed a male figure talking to Sonya. He thought nothing of it, so he walked past, heading for his own vehicle. Once he began fueling, he heard from the other side of the pump, "Well, let me at least call you then."

"No, I'm okay."

"What? Bitch, I know you don't think you all that! Man, gimme somethin' to hit this bitch with."

Johnny peeked above the pumps and saw the guy looking around as if to find something on the ground.

He thought about intervening, but thought, *I don't*

really like that ho anyway. She ratted me out when I tried to slang trees at the bar. Hope he beat her ass. That's when the gas pump stopped too soon, shorting Johnny out of two dollars.

He went inside to check out on the clerk, and as he opened the service station door, he heard: "Johnny help!"

Fuck what you goin' through, thought the abstract accomplice. But when he heard his car alarm screaming, he rushed out the door to find Sonya's assailant looking in his driver-side window, trying to get in. The beef was on!

Man, I wish a muthafucka WOULD! He triple-timed toward the Jack the Ripper wannabe, then scooped the metal trash can that sat between the gas pumps. He mashed the can over Jack's head, and before Jack could even fall good, Johnny grabbed Sonya's purse strap, which Jack had across his shoulder, and pulled Jack's chin into a devilish sledgehammer of a fist. Jack fell forward like an axed tree.

Johnny was intoxicated with anger, surveying his mental archives for the best way to inflict extreme hurt. He stomped Jack a few times, but didn't think that it ailed him enough, so after a few seconds he bent over and grabbed the leg of the would-be car thief. *So you wanna steal from ol' John Dollar, and hurt people and stuff, huh?* Johnny chomped down on the rear of Jack's ankle, then dug deeper into the Achilles tendon with his teeth until he heard Jack sound off in antagonized contralto. Johnny took a deep breath as he bathed in the salubrious wails of Jack's torment, which as far as he knew was the only thing to soothe his conniptuous rage. *Let that be a lesson to ya'!*

Johnny 's cannibalistic moment of triumph was interrupted when Sonya said, "Thank you, Johnny."

He dropped Jack's leg and erected himself. In his pursuit to vanquish the enemy, he had completely forgotten about her even being there. "Huh?"

"I just said, thanks. He had all of my credit cards and everything," Sonya said, lifting her purse from the ground as

E. Scrill/DRUG LORDS

Jack limped away.

Johnny noticed that her shirt had been torn open, and three scratches were on her neck, evidence of Jack's savage thievery--no doubt. Johnny's eyes couldn't help but glide down her almond-colored skin to her bustiered breasts with cocoa crowns that quarter mooned above the brassiere's lace perimeter. *Damn, she was hidin' some shit under that tuxedo shirt.*

"You okay?" she asked, closing her open shirt with one hand, stooping slightly to look into his eyes which were transfixed on her bra.

Johnny blushed like an embarrassed Boy Scout before saying "Oh, I was just tryin' to see if he hurt you."

"Ohhh, that's what you were doing? Well, he just slapped me around a bit and took my chain and purse."

"You want me to go get your necklace before he get away?" Johnny said turning to chase the absconding Jack.

"Wait. It's cool. I saw him shove it in my purse, and I got that back. At least now I don't have to press charges since you prosecuted him yourself."

"Pressin' charges wasn't gon' do too much good unless you knew who he was. It would've helped with the credit cards, though."

"I was just gonna tell them his name."

"Oh, you knew him?" Johnny asked with raised eyebrows.

"No, he just told me his name was Jay when he was tryin' to get my phone number. Guess I should've gave him a fake one, huh?"

"That shit was probably just bullshit talk to get close enough to rob you."

"Yeah, you probably right. Listen, I really appreciate what you did, and I hope you forgive me for gettin' you in trouble that night. I had just had a fight with my--"

"Wait a minute! Didn't you say his name was Jay?" Johnny said as the name finally fit into his grand scheme of things like a key in a lock's tumblers. He turned to see if Jack was still in eyesight, but he had faded into the shadows of the night. *Damn, I let that nigga get away!* "Well, I gotta run. Got some stuff to do, I'll see you at work."

"Okay. Thanks again."

Johnny chirped his keychain to disarm his car's alarm, then hopped in. As he screeched away, he checked his side mirror and saw that he was being hawkeyed by Sonya. *That bitch made me forget to pump the rest of my gas!*

Chapter 13

After leaving Fleetwood's, Mack headed for his crib to catch up on some much-needed rest. He felt like he had done some charity work by even allowing Fleetwood to buy the medication for Sheila. Since he wasn't completely sure the cure would work, he decided not to put the money in his stash yet. He would wait until he saw Sheila up and walking around.

He couldn't stop thinking about the favor Fleetwood asked: to be a part of the new hustle. The look in Fleet's eyes was as solemn as a Dear John letter. As Mack curled up in the fetal position and rested his head on his pillow, he drifted off, hoping that he, too, would be part of the new hustle.

    *   *   *

"Mack, can you hear me?" Johnny said into his cell phone.

"Yeah, what's up? You go by Marlon's yet?"

"Naw, not yet, but I got yo' boy with me."

"Who, Ross?"

"Naw, man. One of the two."

"The two I told you about at the bar?"

114

"Yup. Get my care package together."

"Fall through my crib!"

"I'm in front of Marlon's right now," Johnny said as he turned off Dexter onto Clements. He swerved to avoid hitting a group of young guys walking in the middle of the street. He parked in front of Marlon's and eyeballed the teenagers, who were in his rear-view until they bent the corner. "After I leave here I'll see you."

"Hurry up!"

Johnny smiled after shutting off the phone. He was glad that he didn't send Sonya's call to his voice mail when he saw her number on his caller I.D. Ever since that night at the gas station, he seemed to be in her personal Hall of Fame. She serenaded him with stiff drinks whenever he got a break. And if she happened to catch his eye, she shot him a winning smile. Once he was late for work, so she used that as an excuse to cop his digits from the boss; just to ask if he needed a ride of course. But after that, she would call his phone for flimsy reasons, like the time he was in the restroom out of her sight, gettin' blunted. She claimed that she was worried about not having anyone to walk her to her car at closing time. "You know it's five other bouncers here," Johnny told her.

"What they gon' do if somebody try to get me?" she pouted.

So naturally, when he saw her number on his cell phone on his off day, he didn't think it was anything serious. But after answering, she claimed that the guy who assaulted her was there harassing a few of the dancers. She said she was certain it was him because of his limp.

Johnny thought about the bite he gave Jay that night and said to her, "I owe you big time for this. Good lookin'!" then bolted through four stop signs trying to get to the bar before his co-workers bounced Jay out the door.

Johnny whipped into the parking lot to find Big Mike dragging Jay through the door in a sleeper hold. Ducking his head down to avoid being seen, he watched the gorilla mash

115

Jay's face into the valet shack before throwing him face-first to the cement. When Jay landed, his keys bounced from his pocket. Jay never picked them up, possibly dazed from the abuse.

Damn! He musta really pissed that nigga off, Johnny laughed to himself. He watched Jay quickly get up and limp away while Big Mike watched. Big Mike lifted the keys from the pavement and pocketed them. Excitement cascaded through Johnny at the thought of Jay being stranded. He scrutinized every avenue of his metropolitan mind for a way to pluck the bozo without being seen since he doubted very seriously that Jay would ever be heard from again once he was turned in for the bounty.

Just then, Sonya came through the door on her way to her car.

Hell yeah!

Johnny waited until Jay walked into the alley where his car was parked, then hurried over to meet Sonya at her car.

"Hey," Johnny said as he ran up behind her.

"Oh shit, you scared me," she said as she turned to meet Johnny, then went back to rambling in the console between her two front seats.

"What's goin' on?"

"I know I already owe you , but I need one more favor."

Sonya stood and turned to face Johnny while running her tongue over her front teeth, as if contemplating the vast possibilities of him being in her debt. "And what can I help you with?"

"Can I borrow your car for about a hour? I promise it will be--"

"You crazy! You better ask yo' woman!"

"I ain't got no woman; you know that."

"How I know that? You don't really talk to me...and definitely not about stuff like that."

"Aw, c'mon. This is real important. Look, I'll give

you a hundred dollars, plus take you to dinner where ever you want to eat at.

"Wherever?"

"Yeah, c'mon," he begged.

"You better not be lyin'."

"You know I wouldn't bullshit a woman as fine as you. I been wantin' to holla at you anyway, but I wanted to give it a little time to see if you and your man was gon' get back together. But since you know now, I might at as well tell you that I'm gon' put a smile on yo' face whether you let me use your ride or not. I just hope you can help me right now." He watched as she tried to retard her blush by biting her bottom lip. "Gon on and show that sexy-ass smile," he said watching her lip slip from between her teeth to form a bright smile as he continued to smother her common sense with sweet nothings.

"I got to get back to the bar," she began. "Just be back by the time I get off."

"Cool!"

"Hold up, nigga! Where my money at?" She extended a well-manicured hand.

Just then, Johnny noticed Jay retracing his steps, looking at the ground, obviously searching for his keys. Johnny reached into his pocket and tossed Sonya a folded mass of bills, then hopped behind the wheel of her car. She reached in to jab the keys into the ignition, and a scentacular gust of Dior's Pure Poison flew up Johnny's nostrils. "You a little close to be smellin' good like that," he told her.

Still reaching over him, halfway in the car, she turned her face to him. They were almost close enough to rub noses when he locked on her brown orbs and her rose-colored lips parted to say, "You got a problem with me being close to you?"

"Man, I'll kick it with you later when I pick you up." He stabbed off and watched with his peripheral vision as she backed away watching him.

There that nigga go, he thought as he spotted Jay trying

to flag a cab.

Johnny's adrenaline raced through his body. He paused to allow another car to pass, then watched as Jay started to cross the street behind the passing car.

Johnny stomped the gas pedal in the small Honda.

Jay moved close to the curb, maybe to allow whatever car was coming up behind to pass.

Johnny swerved to the curb behind Jay, continuing to floor the compact machine. The front bumper made contact with Jay's calf muscles, sending him tumbling backward onto the hood of the car. His head bounced off the windshield causing a crack to spider web across the glass. Jay made a frantic attempt to grab the wiper blades as he rolled off the hood onto the pavement. Johnny jerked the car into park, then hopped out.

Looking both ways to make sure that no heroes were making an attempt to save the day, Johnny stepped around to the passenger side where Jay lay. He whipped his belt from the loops, then buckled it around Jay's knees in case he stirred to consciousness. He then popped the trunk, scooped Jay under the legs and around his neck, and dropped him into the waiting compartment.

Jay roused and fluttered his eyelids. He reached up and grabbed hold of Johnny's shirt. Johnny brought all of his weight down into a paramount fist that collided with Jay's chin, causing him to collapse back to the floor of the trunk. Johnny quickly slammed the trunk shut and hopped into the driver seat. He turned the car around and headed for the 'hood.

When Sonya got off, Johnny was there in the parking lot watching as her face beamed child-like promise on Christmas morning. She walked over to the driver side door and reached for the handle.

"You drive my car; I'll drive this," he told her in case his hostage woke and started kicking and screaming. Johnny followed Sonya to her apartment in Southfield, watching

118

closely as she pushed his silvery ho-puller. *Please don't scratch my baby.*

At her apartment, Sonya told Johnny to give her a minute while she showered, then dashed into her bedroom. She came back with her shoulder-length hair in a bun, and a velour robe wrapped around her body.

"You want something to drink before I get in?" she asked.

"Naw, I'm cool."

As soon as Johnny heard the shower come on, he decided to move Jay to his own trunk. But first, he went to the linen closet to grab a few bars of soap.

Delighted that he found a four-pack of Ivory, he took off his socks, then put his shoes back on. He put one sock inside the other, then slid the soap into them both. Johnny planned to beat the dirt off Jay's ass, knowing that once the trunk was popped, Jay would try to spring to freedom.

Johnny hung his make-shift weapon over his shoulder and crept out the sliding doors leading to Sonya's porch. He backed his car to Sonya's trunk, then opened his trunk.

Johnny's heart pumped at light speed, knowing that a nigga inside the trunk would be ready to fight for his life like a cornered rat.

He had to do it.

With his sock in his cocked right hand, he twisted the trunk open with his left.

Jay grabbed frantically at Johnny with both hands, catching hold of his shirt, then trying to pull himself out with the other hand.

Johnny commenced to bouncing the loaded socks off Jay's dome. Jay managed to grab the sock, but Johnny let loose like a demon, drowning Jay with a ferocious torrent of punches that staggered him. Johnny quickly collared Jay, snatching him up, and with a strained hip-toss, flung his upper body into the trunk of the Buick.

Jay's feet dangled down to the car's bumper. Breathing

as if he just ran five blocks, Johnny jumped up, bringing all of his weight down with the trunk's lid into Jay's shins.

"Yaaahhh!" Jay howled in agony.

Johnny repeatedly slammed the trunk on the dangling legs until they disappeared inside between slams.

Once the trunk was closed, Johnny leaned against it and rested for a few seconds before he was startled by Sonya saying, "What's up? You gone?"

"Oh, naw. I was just puttin' some stuff in my trunk I got at the mall today when I was usin' your car."

"Oh. Well, you comin' back in ?"

Johnny looked her from head to toe. She had on an oversized tee-shirt underneath her open robe. Thoughts came to mind of her open shirt that advertised more than a mouthful of cream-colored cleavage. *Yeah I'll come in...and get up under that shirt,* he thought, throwing an arm around her.

"Hey, why didn't you just bite him again?"

Now, after an overnight sex-spree, Johnny had to grab Mack's loot from Marlon so he could turn in Jay and the dough at the same time.

Johnny paused before going in to watch the small crew of knuckleheads pass. He scoped them out from between the houses as a few of them tried to peek into his car on the down low. *Fuck around if you want to, li'l nigga,* he thought coldly before entering the side door.

"Basie, what the fuck you doin' here?" Johnny asked.

"Chillin' with my dog, Marly. Loan me five dollars, big baller."

"Nigga, cut it out." Johnny looked closely at Marlon as he came out of the bathroom. His lips were chalked and his eyes bulged like his head was in a vice. Johnny didn't say anything, but knew the signs of narcosis after years of servin' fiends.

Marlon handed Johnny two bankrolls and said, "Two gee's like it's supposed to be."

"Naw. Should be twenty-five."

E. Scrill/DRUG LORDS

"Uh-oh," Basie said.

"What? Hell naw! Hell naw!" Marlon squawked, twisting his face as if he was really being bamboozled.

Basie sat on the floor picking a gaping nostril with his forefinger and thumb. Being the nuisance that he was, he had to put his two cents in. "Don't do it, Johnny. Don't do it."

"I ain't gon' do nothing; this ain't my loot. That's between him and Mack." Johnny gave Marlon a desecrating stare.

Marlon said, "Man, I need to holla at blood. Maybe he got the sacks mixed up or somethin'."

The Count floated a catastrophic fart, then looked around innocently.

Johnny frowned and said, "Y'all niggas sound like ya wanna be alone." Immediately after, he heard his car's alarm send out an S.O.S., then heard the tires screech off in departure. Sprinting for the door, he stuffed the loot into his pockets. Behind him he heard the Count singing "You've been yay-young hit!"

      *   *   *

Mack rolled down Woodward Avenue thinking of a way to ask Ray for more of the much-needed antibiotics without seeming like that was his only reason for being with her. His relationship with her was turning out to be a lot more than he had bargained for. He never imagined himself being exclusive with any woman, and here he was catching feelings for Ray's young ass. For the last two weeks since she gave him the first bag of capsules, she proved to him that there was a good reason to drop his player's force field and truly give in to the amorous bond that was linking them together.

He first saw her as just another fun time, but then he needed to know about the secret she and her father had so he called himself trying to romance the classified info out of her. That's when she completely vaporized any lasting thoughts that no woman was worthy of an even break from him by

121

putting him on with the cure before he could even crack on her about knowledge of its existence. But, the best part about her was that she just wanted to be all his. How could he deny her?

He didn't have much exposure to a lot of square broads, and never thought he could have any enjoyment with any if he did. She gave it up soon, and he normally would have been leery of hooking up with her again since he thought of a first night fuck as a sign of a woman's tramphood. But, after getting to know Ray, he looked at her as a young woman just going after what she wanted...him. He doubted very seriously that she would give herself like that to just anyone. He could tell that she was the type of woman to completely devote herself to her man, and the fact that she seemed to have such low mileage made things that much better.

Mack saw the way she handled her ex, so he knew she wasn't a pushover, that she could turn on him like a scorned Doberman if he did her wrong. And the way she was giving him her all, he knew if she ever found out about the other chicks, she would surely be pissed. The good thing about that was the fact that she didn't hang around too many other chicks, and the ones she did hang around weren't like any of the broads he usually came across. He knew that even though she was now his woman, he would still be able to find plenty of time to bend over a hoodrat here and there.

As Mack cruised past the Fox theater, he recalled the way Ray lit up when he toyed with her about taking her there. He looked up at the marquee. *Incognito. I know that's gonna be live as hell! Me and my baby will have to hit the mall to get fresh first, though.* He parked and got in the long line to get tickets for the upcoming show.

Chapter 14

Mack stabbed his truck down the Lodge freeway toward the 'hood wondering why Johnny had not yet made contact. He speed-dialed Johnny's number on his cell phone and got the voicemail. Mack had a gut feeling that something was very wrong, so he decided to swing by Marlon's himself.

He came up at Davison Avenue and stopped at the seafood joint since he saw Faye's hooptie out front.

"What's up, baller?" he said to Faye.

She shaped a picture-perfect smile. "Just chillin'. Where you been?"

Mack peeked out the front window at the back of Marlon's crib. A fiend was at the back window. "I been kind of busy, but I ain't forgot about you. I see it's kind of slow today, huh?"

"So-so. It really starts jumpin' again after four."

Mack realized that with Faye's proximity to the spot, she could be a crucial part of his operation; possibly a runner. "How often you be here?"

"Everyday except Sunday. Why you ask?"

"I might need yo' help with a few things...if you don't mind."

"I should've known you wasn't just comin' to holla at a sista. Since you comin' to use me, I'm gon' have to tax you," she joked.

Mack knew she would be ready to assist him in any way she could since it would mean regular contact with him. "Well, dig, I might need you to hold a few sacks for me till Marlon get ready for 'em. Cool?"

"Oh yeah, that ain't nothin'."

"Good lookin'. It might not be today, but what time you get off?"

"I close tonight. If it ain't today, why you need to know what time I get off?" she asked with a hopeful look.

"Just wondering." He thought it might be fitting to scoop her after work and treat her like an executive secretary, but knew he better not make his plans known to her in case something more pressing came up. He knew she would provide excellent service for him for a fee as long as she thought it might be a chance of her muffin being buttered. He also knew that if she began to realize her desires would never materialize she could be a problem, so he would go ahead and break her down like a shotgun to let her know that she would surely get her shot at ghetto stardom as a ballers bitch.

"Damn, that look like that guy you used to be with," Faye said to Mack.

"Where?" Mack jerked his head around to see Johnny hopping into a cab. *What the fuck?* Mack dashed through the door shouting, "Johnny! Yo!" But he was too late. The cab on the other side of the street was out of his throaty range due to the heavy volume of traffic that time of day. Mack watched as the cab bent the corner. He tried Johnny's cell again, but went straight to the recording. He jaywalked over to Marlon's to see what went down.

Marlon answered the door acting nervous.

"What's up?" Mack questioned.

"With what?" Marlon asked.

"Did you give Johnny the money?"

E. Scrill/DRUG LORDS

"Oh, yeah. I just saw him. You ain't see him just now?"

"I saw him, but he ain't see me."

"Aw, damn. He had the money, too," Marlon said, seeming to relax a bit. "Somebody stole his ride from in front of the crib so he said he was gon' jump in a cab."

"Fuck!"

"What?"

"Did he say where he was goin'?"

The Count stuck his head around the corner. "He looked like he was goin' to kick somebody's ass."

Mack jumped at the sound of the Count's voice. "What the fuck he doin' in here? I told you not to let nobody in, nigga!"

"It's just Basie. He straight."

Mack looked at Marlon's dusted lips and saucered eyes. "You been smokin' good, huh?"

"What you mean?"

"You know what I mean. Why you hangin' with Basie if you ain't blowin' stones? I know my money better be right."

Marlon looked to the floor. "It's right."

"I'll see. Where the rest of the sack at?"

Marlon reached into his pocket and pulled out a baggy with five rocks in it.

"How much you give Johnny?"

"I gave him the money."

"Nigga, I said how much."

"I ain't even count it, I just gave him what I had."

"Sound like some bullshit! Let me see that bag."

Mack looked at the stones in the bag, then collared Marlon, pinning him to the wall.

"Nigga, you been chippin' off the rocks?"

"Naw. Hell naw," Marlon said in a shaky voice.

"How the fuck they get so damn small then?"

Sprinkles of spittle rained onto Marlon's face.

"Man, them just the last ones. People bought all the fat

ones first, that's all."

The Count chuckled in the doorway of the dining room as he watched Marlon in his moment of gloom.

Mack felt like Marlon had made a mockery of his intelligence, so he slammed Marlon's back against the wall. "They was all the same size! You saying you and the rocks just in here losin' weight, huh? 'Cause yo' ass definitely gettin' skinny 'round this bitch!"

"I just quit drinkin' beer, that's all," Marlon said as Mack ran his pockets.

"Slang these li'l mu'fuckas two for fifteen, and them chips Johnny got better be right!" Mack gave Marlon a look of disgust. "You skinny as hell! We gon' start callin' yo' ass, Sauce."

The Count held his gut in a fit of laughter, then said, "Yeah, Miriple Sauce!" His catfish lips stretched with every syllable.

Mack heard Angelique moving about upstairs and knew she would be ready to help him blow off some steam. He inhaled deeply to try to calm himself. "Marlon, dig, you need to get back with yo' girl and leave this shit alone. You ain't ready for this."

"Fuck that bitch!" Marlon said with a burst of enthusiasm.

"Look, I'm tellin' you this 'cause I really don't need you. I'll work this bitch myself or just close it down; I'm straight!"

"Chill, dog," Marlon pleaded. "I'll tighten this shit up, just be cool."

"Okay, but if you fuck up my dough, it's comin' out yo' ass!"

The thought of slangin' the cure from the window of the spot crossed Mack's mind, but he knew he would have to get plenty of it in order to set up shop pharmacy style. He thought about the cancerous effect Marlon's habit would have on an operation of that magnitude, so somehow he would have to go.

Maybe Angelique was right. Fuck that smoked-out nigga. Time to get dough! Mack thought coldly as he started toward the door to head upstairs to get a drink and whatever else he might feel like.

"You 'bout to go?" Marlon asked Mack.

"Not yet. I'm 'bout to see if ol' girl got somethin' to drink. I got to take a dump, too, and I ain't 'bout to in that dirty-ass sewer you got in there."

"She-she ain't got nothin' to drink up there," Marlon stammered.

"Well, I still gotta shit."

"Uh-oh," Basie said.

As the door closed and separated Mack from Marlon, Mack could see Marlon's look of despair.

With Angelique under his spell, Mack knew he would be free to utilize her and both flats however he pleased. He knocked twice, then listened as her footsteps came closer.

"What? I know you ain't lose your key again, Marlon," she grouched.

"It's Mack."

The door flew open and Angelique's charged smile welcomed him in.

Angelique's short shorts and tank top was saying a lot to Mack's dick. Even with the scarf on her head, she had an appetizing look about her.

"What you in here doin'?" Mack asked as he slapped her ass.

"Waitin' for you," she said with a broad grin.

Mack decided to turn on the juice to confirm his position since Marlon would be gone soon. He stroked her cheek with his forefinger. "So that's why you lookin' so good today, huh?"

"Yeah," she giggled like a schoolgirl.

"I don't believe you; I think you all dolled-up for Marlon," he said, knowing she probably heard Marlon curse her and would have both barrels loaded.

"Didn't he just say 'Fuck me?' I told you before that I don't mess around with him anymore. I just got a check-up, and ain't tryin' to catch nothin' from that bum. You the one act like you ain't got no time for a sista."

"Why you think I'm here? I thought we was gon' work on gettin' rid of him?" Mack watched Angelique show her sparkling thirty-twos. Her nipples poked dents in her top from the inside. "You still wanna work with me?"

"Yeah, you know I do."

"I don't know nothin' unless you show me."

"How am I s'posed to do that? You don't never come around."

"You know I got a woman, right?"

"Yeah, I know."

"I'm just bein' honest. You know it's best if we start things out right."

"That's true. It's good that you bein' honest, too; I like that."

"So that won't be a problem with us, will it?"

"How is it gon' be a problem? I'm down for you."

"I'll see." Mack unzipped his fly and freed his magnificence. He knew just because she claimed to have had a check-up that she wasn't necessarily ZGP-free, but he was now plugged with the cure and wasn't as worried as before.

Their eyes locked for a few seconds, then she began her descent to her knees. Mack watched the top of her head as she rubber-necked with vigor, once again proving that Marlon's terminal love life had been euthanized.

*　　　　*　　　　*

Marlon shushed the Count and tried to listen for any sounds through the floor that might reveal the going-ons upstairs…to no avail.

The Count frowned and said, "Don't be shushin' me, nigga! I can talk. You shoulda been doin' some push-ups instead of bullshittin' all day, then you coulda hit that nigga up-side his head."

"Shut-up!"

"Don't get mad at me, I ain't do it. That nigga gone now. Shit, you shoulda acted bad when he was down here, then he wouldn't be up there feelin' nasty."

"Just 'cause he up there don't mean he doin' nothin'. He just takin' a shit."

"Yeah, a shit on yo' relationship."

"Nigga, he just got up there; you trippin'. He'll be right back."

"Yeah, okay," The Count said, looking at the corroded calculator watch on his wrist and shaking his head. "I don't know, dog. I wouldn't want no playa like Mack alone wit' my poontang this long. He probably stretchin' that thang out."

Marlon chewed the inside of his jaw as the Count painted an antagonizing portrait in his head. He knew that Angelique would gladly raise her ankles to her earlobes for Mack. Marlon felt defenseless. *Why did the footsteps stop in the living room? What the fuck are they doin' up there?* "Man, you gotta to," he told Basie.

"Why you throwin' me out? I was just bullshittin'. You ain't throw Mack out. I still got money to spend; gimme two of them thangs."

As Marlon went for his pocket, he could feel storm clouds gathering inside his eye sockets. He ran to the back, acting like he heard something at the window so the Count couldn't see him cry. He ducked into the bathroom and slammed the door. The Count's footsteps were close behind.

"Hey, man, you alright?" the Count questioned.

"Yeah, I'm cool." *I'm gon' fix both of them muthafuckas!*

*　　　　　*　　　　　*

"Hello," Ray said into her cell phone.

"Yeah, this Ninean. I was callin' to see if you felt like

129

hittin' the mall with me."

"I don't care. You 'bout to come get me?"

"Yeah. I'll be there in five minutes."

Ray figured that Ninean needed to talk or just didn't want to be alone. She understood how a woman could feel after a sexual assault from being there with another of her girlfriends after such an incident. Since she wasn't doing anything anyway, she figured she might as well get in good with Mack's sister, also hoping to discover some juicy new info about Mack.

Ray rushed through the side door to Ninean's car. She expected Ninean to be blue, but she was just the opposite.

Right off, Ray noticed a Styrofoam cup in the cup holder, and a brewed fragrance in the air. "What you drinkin' on?"

Ninean snatched a fifth-sized bottle of gin from under the front seat and passed it to Ray. Ray looked into Ninean's glossy eyes before she took it. Ray saw that the bottle was half-empty and assumed that Ninean had been trying to drink her problems away.

"Girl, I don't know if you should be drinking like this after what happened to you," Ray began. "This is too much for just you."

"I didn't drink all that. I vamped that from Mack's room; that was his. But I'm straight on that bullshit that happened; them niggas will get theirs. I ain't even got to worry 'bout that. I'm just havin' a drink to mellow-out a bit before I do some shoppin'."

"Oh, my fault," Ray laughed. "I thought you did all this yourself. I was 'bout to say…" The two laughed for a minute before Ray said, "Well, I guess Mack won't mind if we have a little taste." Ray looked around for something to pour her shot into.

"You got another cup?"

"I'll stop by the store so you can grab one."

They pulled off and stopped at a gas station on the

E. Scrill/DRUG LORDS

Southfield service drive. Ray pulled her shades from her purse seeing that the sun was beginning to set, but was still bright.

"Damn, don't go rob the place," Ninean joked.

Ray would sometimes flirt with guys while out even if she had no intention on talking to them, but made a mental note to stay on her P's and Q's while with Ninean. She could tell that Ninean was cool, but didn't really know if she could trust Ninean not to tell Mack if she got her flirt-on.

Several cars on the service drive tooted horns at Ray as she strutted back toward Ninean's car. She tried not to switch too much as one of the guys pulled into the gas station to holla at her.

Damn, not now! Ray thought, trying to hurry and get back into the car.

"Can I talk to you for a minute?" asked a brown-skinned face from the window of a dilapidated Caprice Classic.

"No, that's okay. I got a man," Ray declined.

As the Caprice stabbed back onto the service drive, Ray hopped back into Ninean's car.

"Do it girl; I see you." Ninean joked.

Ray poured out a fourth of the grapefruit juice she purchased, then topped the juice bottle off with gin. She had been drinking a lot more lately than she ever had in the past, and was planning on pumping her brakes. But, every time she got with Mack, there were drinks so she would take one more. Now, with his sister, she was about to hit the mall, so she had one more.

They sipped and listened to the top eight countdown on the radio. They hopped on the Southfield freeway and headed for Northland Mall.

Ninean and Ray jumped on a sale at Marshall Fields, grabbing two outfit's apiece. When they approached the counter, Ray reached for her purse, but Ninean insisted on footing the bill for all four hook-ups.

Okay, cool with me, Ray thought as she watched

E. Scrill/DRUG LORDS

Ninean try to be discreet while pinching off a thick bankroll that was stuffed into her purse. In turn, Ray paid to get their nails done, and for the food they demolished at the Food Court. While eating, Ray's cell phone gave a muffled ring from inside her small handbag.

"Hello," she answered.

"Hey, baby. How's everything?"

"Oh, hi, Daddy. Everything is fine. How are you?"

"I'm all better now. What about Pat? Have you been giving her the doses like I told you to?"

"Oh yeah. She's getting around again. I think she will be a hundred percent shortly."

"That's good. Hey, what about your friend, the one I gave you the--"

"Oh, she's fine too. You got anymore?"

"I thought you said she was fine?"

"Yeah, she is, but..."

"Look, Ray. I told you how serious that situation was. I don't want you messing around trying to help if that's what you're thinking of."

"I know, I know. It's just that so many people have that...problem that we can help. I just think we should be doing more, that's all."

"There is no 'us' when it comes to that. That is something that I am working out, and I want you to forget about trying to save the world. It's just too dangerous. Okay?"

There was a few second pause before Ray answered with, "Okay, Daddy." She knew that if she could somehow get more of the medicine, she would be able to put a smile on her Mack's face again, and she loved the thought of doing that. She knew of no other way to make him that happy. He seemed to be able to get everything else he wanted, except out of the dope game. And that's the main thing she wanted to see if at all possible; especially since it was something that he wanted, too.

E. Scrill/DRUG LORDS

She would just have to be truthful with her father and tell him that Mack sold the other stuff he gave to her. It wasn't like he wouldn't be her father anymore.

She didn't exactly know how to cut into her old man for more of the cure, but knew better than trying to do it over the phone.

"Well, I guess you're right again, Daddy," she agreed until she could find another way to put the squeeze on him.

"I know I am. That's why I'm the Daddy, and you're the baby."

"I ain't no baby."

"You will always be my baby."

"Yeah, whatever. Well, I'm at the mall with my friend, Ninean. You remember her don't you? Mack's sister?"

"Oh, yeah, Mack, your new boyfriend. How are things with you two anyway?"

"Fine. He told me to tell you 'Hi' whenever I talked to you again," she lied in an attempt to gain Mack a few stripes with Pops.

"Oh, okay. Well, tell him I said hi, too. Maybe I was wrong about him."

The comment brought a smile to Ray's face. She knew if her father accepted Mack, there was a better chance of him being plugged with loads of the cure. She doubted he would worry so much about Mack's safety. Jubilant thoughts of her helping Mack out of the dope game skated through her mind. She felt one step closer since Pops now seemed to be trying to accept Mack.

"Yeah, he is really okay once you get to know him. Maybe we can come down there to spend a little time with you."

"No, not now. Maybe later on. Listen, I almost forgot to tell you: I put a package in your room, and I might need you to do something for me with it, but I'll let you know."

"Okay, well I'll talk to you later. I love you. Bye."

A package? I bet it's some more of that stuff! Well,

133

E. Scrill/DRUG LORDS

whatever it is, I am going to tear that room apart looking for it.!

Chapter 15

Johnny stabbed Sonya's bell with his forefinger as he watched the cab speed away. He knew she would be getting ready for work and would be rushing, so he planned to drop her off and use her car.

She answered the door wearing a robe and slippers. Johnny stormed into the apartment and snatched the phone receiver from its cradle.

"Hello," Ross answered.

"Yeah, this Johnny."

"What's poppin'? You ready to make that happen?"

"I had the nigga and lost him. Somebody stole my fuckin' car, man!"

"Oooh, that hurts. Where you at?"

"At Sonya's."

"From the bar?"

"Yeah."

"Straight up? Do yo' thang, homie! Did you tell Mack yet?"

"Naw. I tried to call him, but my phone keep roamin'. Well, dig, let me kick it with her for a minute; I'll hit you back, but be ready."

135

E. Scrill/DRUG LORDS

When Johnny looked up at Sonya, he could see that she already got an earful of his disastrous day and was headed toward him with a concerned look on her face.

"You okay?" she asked.

"Yeah, I'm cool."

"I can call in; I got a few sick days left if you need me."

"Naw, I'll be okay. I just might need to use your car again if it's cool with you."

He watched her Creole face as she looked to the floor. "Johnny, I will help you as much as I can, but you know you cracked my windshield last time I let you use my car..."

"I know, I know. I got that. Just let me know how much it cost."

"Okay, but please be careful. I can't be without transportation."

"Don't even worry. If anything goes wrong, I'll cash you out. I just need to get around for a minute."

"Now see, if you was my man, maybe I could help you get a car or something."

"Well, we can kick it later about all that, right now I got some serious shit goin' on."

"Okay," she said while undoing her robe and letting it fall to the floor. She gazed at him hungrily. "You look like you could use a little cheering up before I get dressed to go to work; I got forty-five minutes."

Johnny reached for her, then his cellphone rang. "Mack! Where you at?"

"At Marlon's. What happened?"

"Somebody stole my car. I think it was them little niggas down the street."

"Where is ol' boy?"

"He was in the car."

"Damn! Where you at?"

"In Southfield."

"You got the bread Marlon gave you?"

136

E. Scrill/DRUG LORDS

"Yeah, but that nigga five-hundred in the hole. He was in there gettin' keyed with Basie."

"I knew he was on some bullshit! I'm gon' go down there and stomp his ass!"

"Oh, you upstairs, huh?"

"Just chillin'. That nigga over wit'! Keep yo' phone on. I'll holla back."

*   *   *

After tearing the bedroom apart, Ray finally found the stash under her dresser. Her eyes bulged at the baggy stuffed with the medicine. She figured she had enough to cure over a dozen infected people.

Mack is gon' love this! she smiled.

After a nap, she heard a knock at the side door, then her mother answer. She hurried through the kitchen when she heard Mack's voice.

He was leaning against the sink with a large shopping bag in hand.

"What's all that?" Ray asked through a gigantic cheese.

"I got us a little somethin' to wear to the concert tonight. You game?"

"Man, quit playin'. You know I'm game."

She watched with diligence as Mack yanked two linen short sets from the bag. Hers was tan and his powder blue.

"Hurry and try it on in case it don't fit. I did the best I could with tellin' the girl in the store what size you was. If you need shoes, we got to bounce now to get 'em."

"I got some to go with that. Let me see how fat you think I am," she said as she grabbed the outfit and broke for her bedroom.

By the time Mack got to the door, she was dressed and posing in the mirror.

Ray closed the door after hearing the stairs creak under her mother's feet.

"Perfect!" She smiled and took a deep breath of

E. Scrill/DRUG LORDS

Mack's Reaction, by Kenneth Cole. "So, who we goin' to see tonight?"

"It's a surprise."

"You shouldn't keep secrets from me."

"I don't think you'll have a problem with it once we get there."

"Oh, okay. Well, I guess I'll have to save your surprise for later, too."

"I guess so."

"Fine by me," she said before she was pushed onto the bed. She looked into Mack's eyes as he climbed on top of her. His face was smothered with sugary pecks as a reward for the upcoming outing.

"Damn, I guess I need to grab concert tickets more often."

"Yup!"

"Can I take a shower here before we go?"

"I think I can swing that if I can get in with you."

Ray watched as Mack undressed, then peeped into the hallway to make sure that the coast was clear. She knew her mother was getting better, but still stayed in bed mostly. Her only fear was that they would be caught in the nude if her mother had to rush into the bathroom.

She normally didn't take risks such as these with Pat home, but the risk seemed to make everything all the more thrilling.

After showering, Ray and Mack left the humid, steamed-filled bathroom and speed-dressed. Then, it was off to the Fox.

They strutted through the crowded lobby, polished and shining. All eyes seemed to be on them. Once again, Ray watched the effects of Mack's planetary reputation as he got pounds from homies and "hellos" from obviously envious females.

Ray didn't sweat any of the desperate flirts from the chicks; she felt completely secure in her situation.

E. Scrill/DRUG LORDS

They sat watching the show, enthralled by the sorcery of the musical performers.

As the rest of the auditorium stood in ovation, Ray reached for the plastic baggy she had squirreled away in her tits.

She looked over at Mack who was taking his seat, and rushed him, lipsticking his cheek. When he looked back at her, she pointed down to his lap where she had planted the capsules with pick-pocket swiftness.

He snatched up the baggy, stuffed it in his pocket, and looked around as he tried to deflate his monstrous grin.

Ray leaned back in her seat, watching Mack as he tried his best to act like he was unaffected and still watching the show. It tickled her the way he tried to cloak his emotions, as if he was above all feeling.

She tapped him on the shoulder, and as he slowly turned to face her, he lost his frosty composure, joining her in a hearty laugh before showing his gratitude with a sloppy tongue kiss.

Ray knew as she tasted the liquor on Mack's tongue, that she would have to find a way to let her father know what was really going on with the capsules she gave Mack. *Got to just tell Daddy the truth. All he can do is understand how much I care for my man and why I need to help him. I pray Daddy just lets Mack work with him; everything would be so much better.*

*   *   *

Ross sat in his girlfriend's Oak Park condo awaiting Johnny's call. The situation sounded like it might finally be his chance to crack some heads. He couldn't wait to crack some heads.

He had just got done cleaning his chrome nine-millimeter. He used his shirt-tail to handle the bullets to keep from leaving prints from his bony fingers. He carefully twisted each hollow-point into a turd that was in a baby diaper

139

he lifted from his neighbor's garbage. He adopted that practice after learning from a special on cable television about the poisonous properties of human excrement. He figured that if the hole from one of his poo-poo pellets didn't kill, then a bacterial infection would.

After loading two clips with the booby-trapped slugs, he dressed in all black night-gear, which was worn only when he planned to do dirt. And he lived to do dirt.

When he hurt people, it wasn't for the same reasons as Johnny; Ross did it just because. He was nuts; the type of nigga that might play with gasoline in a blazing inferno. He didn't give a damn.

He didn't harbor the fears many did. Fears of actually getting hurt or killed while committing dangerous acts. He figured if it was his time to go, then he was just hit. So he would try most anything he could imagine without getting locked up.

Rival drug dealers hated his guts. A few even tried to have him killed just to get rid of him. His name struck fear in their entrepreneurial hearts, knowing that he soon would come and take, sometimes without a gun, just by his maniacal reputation.

He once invaded a crack house in his 'hood ran by a dopeman called Black. Once inside, Ross told Black's worker, "Look, you got a gee, so give me that and I'll split the dope with you. Just tell your boss I took everything. Oh, but I need that house heater, too." The worker bit hard on the deal, happy that he didn't have to suffer any physical pain.

Ross took the cash and the gun, then went ten blocks over and used Black's gun to stick up another of Black's money spots. This time he pulled the heater since that worker was new to the area and knew nothing of Ross's way of getting down...until he was pistol-whipped senseless.

Black was never again seen after telling his workers that he was going to check Ross about the robberies.

Ross's bovine sweet thang, Tasha, swore to the

authorities that Ross was with her the entire day that Black disappeared.

Ross leaned back on the couch watching television. He was growing impatient. He had been waiting, trying to stay out of trouble until Mack was released. Now he was out, and Ross was ready to get busy. He always felt like his homies were leaving him out on most of the action. Actually, they were. Mack knew to only unleash Ross when the situation called for extra grimy measures. He was paid well, but hated the waiting periods.

While surfing the channels, he reached into his pants and began to juggle his balls. He began to wish Tasha was home to keep him company. He loved her dearly. With her he was as soft as butter, a pussycat. Tasha and Mack were the only ones he really listened to. He never told her about the things he did in the streets knowing that she would just flog him with one of her profane verbal assaults.

He stood only five-six, with a bony frame. His inch and a half afro was just long enough to grip for braiding.

Although Tasha was fat and looked like she had her ass where her stomach should be, Ross felt her lovin' was that deal. He needed no one else and treated her in a chivalrous manner, pampering her with long-stemmed roses, and even resurrecting her to cunnilingual mornings until his face was plastered with vaginal goo.

Ross heard Tasha's key enter the lock and jumped to his feet. As soon as she walked in, he seized her in his bony arms. They butterfly kissed as he slow-danced her to the couch. He stretched out, laying his head on her lap and she played with his ears. He stuck a blunt in his mouth and she blazed it up. He passed it to her, then the phone rang.

"What up, dog? You ready?" Johnny asked.

"Yup."

"Meet me on Fenkell, at the candy store."

Ross grabbed Tasha's keys, then kissed her as he left. He stabbed her black Escort toward the 'hood, ready for whatever.

Flying down Schaeffer, he saw Johnny's Regal bend the corner at Grove. He turned behind it, creeping. He stayed a block behind, trying to see where the car would stop.

It was times like these that he wished he had a cellphone. Usually, he didn't feel the need for one. Now, he wasn't really sure what move to make. *Fuck it! Might as well play to win,* he thought.

He watched the car turn onto Stansbury. Ross stopped for a few seconds to allow the driver time to get out in case he was parking.

As he turned the corner, he saw the car parked in front of the third house on his right. The driver was just sticking his legs out the door.

Ross cruised by and parked four houses down from the car and watched his rear view mirror as the driver and the passenger walked to the rear of the Regal. They jimmied the trunk open with a screwdriver, then the driver disappeared into the trunk as the passenger jumped back.

He saw a figure leap out and chase the passenger two houses toward Grove before going back to the car and hop into the driver's seat.

Ross rolled down his window, and as the Regal started to pass, he unloaded his nine into it.

He watched as it fishtailed around the corner. *I know I had to hit that nigga,* he thought as he started toward the candy store where Johnny was waiting.

142

Chapter 16

After leaving the Fox theater, Mack thought about Big Stan. He hadn't talked to his old friend since he copped dope from him three days ago, and then Stan's health seemed to be declining. He had lost over sixty pounds and had a blazing fever.

Mack never spoke anything of the cure to him since he wasn't sure if he would be able to get more. If Stan found out that Mack had a cure and sold it to someone else, the outcome would have been ugly.

But since Ray came through with more capsules, Mack knew she could get more after that was gone.

Mack's thoughts of cocaine now gave him a feeling of dread...as if he were allergic to it. He didn't want to sell another stone after he pushed the last of what he had. He had worked so hard to get his moneyspot to where it was; doing twenty-five hundred a day, but was ready to scatter his clientèle into the wind without a second thought.

He didn't want to be bothered with Marlon anymore either. He had already been devising a plan to rid himself, and the flat of Marlon without causing him any physical harm, which would bring too much heat. And heat he didn't want in his new hustle.

Since he knew that no one else had knowledge of the cure, the authorities would have a bitch of a time prosecuting him, if he ever got pinched. But he knew he should be able to hustle his pockets obese before he even got hot.

He knew he would still be selling dope, but the new product wasn't poison. After all, he would now be saving lives instead of sponging the essence out of folks using cooked-up 'cain. He dropped Ray off at his house, then swung by Stan's. Normally, he would have called first, but knew Stan wouldn't want time wasted talking with his life-force diminishing. So why burn up the phone lines?

Mack pulled into the driveway behind Stan's Caddy truck and pranced to the porch jabbing the bell with a knuckle. Duke answered the door with indo-red eyes.

"Where fat boy at?" Mack asked.

"He in the bed. You know he all fucked up, man. He really don't want nobody seein' him like that. Hold up, I'll let him know you're here."

Mack watched Duke disappear into one of the back rooms. He knew Stan would have turned him away, being in his shriveled state and all. Mack decided to deal with Stan's pride later and headed for the room Duke ducked into.

He collided with Duke as he passed through the doorway. Stan perked to the upright position in his bed at the sight of Mack.

"What's up, man?" Stan began with his face twisted into an irritated frown. His once round jowls were now reduced to just loose skin that draped from his face like a bulldog's. "Why you runnin' up in my room like you the police? You know you supposed to hit me up before you fall through here!"

"Chill out!" Mack said before he turned to Duke and said, "Let me kick it with him for a minute." After watching Duke cautiously back out of the room, Mack turned back to Stan. "How bad is your fever?"

E. Scrill/DRUG LORDS

"Last time I checked, it was a hundred-three. Why?"

"Peep this out: I got something that can help you. You can't tell nobody 'bout this shit 'cause we the only ones with it."

"I'm listenin'," Stan said.

Mack pulled out a pill bottle with enough capsules to bring Stan back from the brink of death. "These antibiotics I got the hook-up on should straighten you out in a few weeks."

"Man, you bullshittin'," Stan said with a cough.

"Look, man, I ain't gon' come 'round here playin' with you like this."

"Okay, but what's the ticket?" Stan questioned with the vigilance of a deer.

Mack thought about Stan's bloated pockets, and at first was going to tax him, but then he looked over at his homeboy's weakened condition and knew he would feel bad to squeeze him...being on his deathbed and all. But, before Mack could say a word, Stan wheezed, "Don't even worry about it, dog. I told you before if you had a cure, you could write your own ticket. I can't go out like this. You can have the house on St. Clair, just help me. I don't even care what you charged everybody else. I ain't got time to be tryin' to jew you down. I can't take this shit no more!"

"Don't even worry 'bout it, playa." Mack tossed the pill bottle to his dying friend. Even though Mack never quoted a price, guilt gnawed at his conscience as if he had been part of Hitler's regime.

Mack told Stan the in's and out's of the capsules, then decided to float through the 'hood. He knew Fleetwood wanted bad to be down with the new program, but would never blow up his phone with nagging calls.

As Mack coasted up Fleet's block, his guilty feelings were canceled out by the refreshing sight of Fleet and his sister sitting on the porch.

Fleetwood ran to the middle of the street and hopped into the truck with Mack and they drove to the liquor store where all the fellas in the 'hood congregated.

Fleetwood grabbed a bottle of champagne and popped the cork. He took a swig, then passed it to Mack.

"So I see sis' is doin' better," Mack said.

"She gettin' there. But my mother, man, if you would've saw her at church."

"She got down on the testimony tip, huh?"

"Then did the Holy Dance on one leg. We need a bus load of that shit, young fella."

"I wish I had it. I'm workin' on it though."

"Well, when we get it, I got a crew to flip it. We don't ever have to tell them what it is."

"They must be young."

"Don't they make the best workers?"

"With 'cain. They might get us hot if they do some dumb shit. We got to make this work right the first time; ain't no trophies for second place. If I get a load of this, I want to be through wit' it before the Feds find out it even exists."

"I feel you. See, I was thinkin' 'bout doin' it off the pager. Once the custos get referred to us, we get the bread, then send 'em to the spot where the young niggas at."

"They won't trust that. It will already be hard enough to believe that it is a cure. That sound too much like a old con game. I was thinkin' 'bout just havin' the custos go by the spot with a password. We change the password every week to make sure we ain't hot. Nobody ain't gon' be comin' more than once anyway."

"Once a nigga get straight and don't need us no more, he liable to rat us out just to beat a parking ticket!"

Mack chuckled, then said, "Think about it like this: these niggas dyin'. We the only salvation they got. Would you rat us out?" Mack asked, sitting back in his seat.

"You probably right 'cause the only ones that's gon' be able to afford this will have better sense than the baseheads."

In the next two weeks, Mack allowed the traffic at Marlon's to dry up, while at the same time sending Angelique out to hospitals to post up and watch the parking lots for ZGP victims hopping out of lavish vehicles. She was schooled on how to screen and interview their caregivers to make sure that the victim was sittin' on sufficient funds.

Angelique would first compliment the caregiver on their top-notch taste in wheels, then explain that she worked at a dealership that sold that certain type of car, and would offer a price for it. Most times the caregiver at that point would let her know that they were there to help a loved one receive medical attention, and that the car belonged to the uninterested victim. She would then allow the caregiver to aid the ailing person to the emergency entrance to sit in the congested waiting area where the smell of puke and diarrhea persevered from the many skeletal ZGP victims that were tap dancing blindfolded on the brim of Death's scalding cup of joe. With no hope of a cure, or the necessary toilets to occupy all the suffering patients, most would rather go back home instead of suffering in the cramped torture chamber. So they would return to their cars after about an hour. Angelique would then pitch hope to a hopeless situation.

With the caregiver now irritated, she would have to talk fast, revealing her real motive and why they had to be screened the way they did. Out of ten victims, only two declined to take the pager number. She didn't worry about the doomed nonbelievers since she changed rental cars and hospitals everyday. The number went to a pager carried by Fleetwood since he would be the one actually handling the business transactions.

*   *   *

Angelique sat on the living room sofa with Marlon, sipping from her glass of liquid courage. She knew the task, which was put together by her and Mack, would not be easy. Even though she didn't care much for Marlon, setting him up wasn't as easy as it sounded.

She couldn't help but notice the way he lit up when

147

around her. She felt like a monster. He only wanted to make her happy, and now she was going to put herself completely out of his reach. She swallowed deep from the glass.

The shirt he had on was from two years ago, and hung from his bony frame like a hand-me-down from a fat person. He had lost so much weight in the last few months that Angelique began to wonder if ZGP was the cause, but after realizing that he had none of the symptoms, she knew it was his crack diet.

He flashed his buttery smile every chance he got, as if he didn't know that his teeth were now cigarette-smoked yellow. The fade Count Basie gave him was tired, with an unblended line around his head and an uneven line-up. Marlon could've done better blindfolded using his left hand. Sweat caused the back and sides to nap up into tight little beads. His hair even looked dusty and abrasive enough to scratch her hand if she touched it. Stress had long ago devoured his widow's peak.

Though he tried to douse himself with cologne, he looked funky so Angelique kept her distance. But still, she felt too sorry for him to get rid of him.

Then, thoughts of Mack being angry with her started to rise. She knew he wasn't her man, but still wanted to keep him happy, even if she did only get to see him twice a week nowadays, and even then she was getting her knees dirty. But she saw more promise in blowin' Mack like the wind than dealing with Marlon on any level.

She gulped the remainder of her drink. *Hold up! What the hell am I feelin' sorry for yo' corroded ass for? You was down there big timin' with them crackhead bitches! I ain't seen none of that dope money either. Nigga you outta there!*

With an offense in place to counter her slutty antics, she poured another drink, and then told Marlon, "Look, you gotta get ready to go; Mack 'bout to come over." She watched as his face reflected the hurt of her words.

"What the fuck you mean? He bringin' some dope by

148

here?"

"Naw. He just comin' to chill wit' me. I ain't say nothin' when you was gettin' yo' freak on with them ho's downstairs so don't sweat me." Knowing that the beef was on, she eased into the dining room toward the house phone Mack had turned on in her name. She dialed 911, and then continued to argue, knowing that the operator would just trace the call and send a squad car to the house.

"Fuck that shit!" Marlon yelled, stepping closer to Angelique.

"Don't hit me, Marlon," she said, making sure it was loud enough for the operator to hear.

Tears pooled in Marlon's eyes as he called Angelique bitches and sluts, unwittingly revealing her whoredom to no one but the 911 operator whose job was to record everything said as long as the call was connected.

Angelique sprang to the window when she heard the officer's knock at the door. "The side door is open," she told them. After cutting off the cordless phone, she dashed into the bedroom where she quickly changed into the torn shirt from the attempted rape.

She heard Marlon rambling around outside her room door before he said, "I'm gon' bust that nigga's head this time!" She held her ear to the door and listened as the police officers charged into the flat, obviously subduing Marlon since she could hear them yelling, "Drop the bat or I'll blow your fuckin' head off!"

"I-I thought y'all was somebody else," Marlon's voice said.

"Where is the woman that called?" she heard another voice ask.

Angelique stepped from the room to see two overweight officers. One searching Marlon's pockets, while the other came toward her asking, "You all right ma'am?"

"I'm okay now," she said, playing the battered spouse role.

E. Scrill/DRUG LORDS

"Did he hit you?" one officer asked.

"I ain't touch her," Marlon yelled.

"Shut the fuck up," the officer screamed at Marlon, mashing his face against the wall.

"Angie, tell him I ain't hit you," Marlon yelled, trying to turn his head to face her, but the officer took Marlon's struggle as resisting arrest and tenderized his rib cage with a fist.

The other officer escorted Angelique to the dining room table to talk to her where Marlon's abuse was out of view. As she gave her false testimony, she could hear a beatdown ensuing in the other room.

"Well, since you refuse to press charges, we will have to take him to the station for resisting arrest and possibly domestic abuse. Since he cursed at you, he can be charged with verbal abuse, and the State may decide to pick up the charges. But, he will still have to spend twenty-three hours in the precinct--just a little cooling off period before he can make bail."

Angelique watched as Marlon was dragged off complaining about how tight the cuffs were. He now had two green speed knots erupting from his forehead. Angelique simply ignored him, unable to make eye contact as he asked, "Why, baby?" while being stuffed into the back seat of the squad car.

While Marlon was being detained, she had Mack take her to the police station where she filed a restraining order which he would receive in his cell.

Mack spent a few hours with her that night, drinking, talking, and undressing. She felt better while he was there, but knew she would soon be lonely as hell.

Chapter 17

Marlon lay in the small cell at the Tenth Precinct. It felt like he had bedsores from the stone slab he lay on. When he shifted from his side to his back, he only felt relief for about ten minutes before the small of his back began to feel numb. He propped his head up on a roll of toilet paper he found on the sink and received temporary relief from the pain in his neck.

His cell was bumpin' from the piss stew that was marinating in the broken toilet. He felt like he had been strategically placed in that cell for giving the officers a hard time. He could smell the aroma of weed coming from one of the other cells. He knew if he had a rock he could better deal with the tortuous situation he had been crossed into.

"Hey, pass that weed down here," he whispered loudly, but heard nothing except a toilet flushing a few cells down.

As he paced the floor--his laceless tennis shoes making a sucking noise while flopping off his feet--he thought of where he would sleep when he got out since he wasn't allowed to be within fifty feet of his home. He could only think of his mother's couch, but she lived on the east side, and that would be too far from Angelique.

Even though Marlon knew she was the cause of his incarceration, he couldn't manage to free his mind of her. Carnivorous thoughts of her and Mack locked up like humping poodles ate away at his sanity.

Amorously bankrupt and thirsty, he leaned his wiry

frame against the bars. "Turnkey! Can we get some water in here?"

No answer.

He could feel his armpits getting sweaty. His deodorant was wearing off and soon he would be musty. He yelled for the turnkey again, but again he got no results. "I'm gon' sue y'all stinkin' asses for havin' me in this inhumane shit when I get outta here! I'm a boss! I got lawyers and shit!" he threatened, but still no results.

"What you in here for?" a voice from the neighboring cell asked.

"Man, I was gettin' money, and my spot got knocked," he lied

"Damn, that's fucked up. Where you from anyway?" the voice asked.

"Over off Dexter. I got a spot right on Clements."

"That's you?"

"Yup. You been through there before?"

"Naw. What they call you?"

"Marlon."

"Oh, okay. I must got the wrong spot. The one I'm thinkin' 'bout is a nigga named Mack's."

"He was down wit' me for a minute, but I do my own thang now." Marlon proudly deceived.

"So you bossed up on his ass, huh?"

"Hell yeah! I can't be sharin' my bread like dat; I'm too greedy." *Damn, I don't even know who I'm talkin' to. I better chill.* "You from that way?"

"I'm from everywhere really."

"What they call you?"

"Smooth."

"Naw, you ain't from my way. I been gettin' dough around there forever, and I know everybody in the 'hood," Marlon bragged, once again feeling comfortable in his misleading moment.

"Runnin' thangs, huh?"

E. Scrill/DRUG LORDS

"Man, hell yeah! If a nigga wanna roll in my 'hood, he gotta get my blessings first! That's how I get down."

"That's gangsta!"

"That's what I'm talkin' 'bout. This is mob shit!"

Marlon's falsehoods were interrupted when the turnkeys finally brought in a pitcher of water and Styrofoam cups.

As the turnkey sat Marlon's cup on the bars and moved to fill the cup at the next cell, he noticed that his was already filled with water.

Them fat bastards that brought me in must've told this ho to give me some toilet water. "Yo, why you ain't get my water out the pitcher like everybody else's?" he quizzed the female turnkey.

"That's just so I don't have to make two trips. This pitcher ain't gon' hold enough water to fill all y'all cups, so you got the cup I filled when I filled the pitcher."

"Why just mines then?" he asked like he knew he caught her in a lie.

"'Cause you in the first cell," she answered sharply, apparently getting tired of his questions.

"Naw, naw, I ain't buyin' that," Marlon said as he shook his head.

"Well, don't drink it then," the turnkey said in a stank way.

Marlon began to really get thirsty as she walked back past his cell and passed through the doors from which she came. He looked at the cup, then peeked into it. *Naw, hell naw! They ain't gettin' me like that!*

Marlon jumped to the bars an hour later when the turnkey came to bring sandwiches with more water. She left a bag on his bars, then continued to the next cell.

"Why you didn't give me no new water?"

"Cause you still got a full cup."

"This water ain't cold no more," he complained.

"Your cup is full, so I can't put nothin' in it."

153

E. Scrill/DRUG LORDS

Marlon emptied the water into the sink, then posted up at the bars.

"The pitcher is empty now," she said, walking past Marlon as he stood holding the cup out like a destitute panhandler.

"Fuck it then, drink that stanky water! I'm gon' be poppin' bottles of Moet soon as I get out," he fronted. Marlon sat on the cold slab of cement and started to choke down the dry bologna sandwich he had.

"Hey, Smooth, you got some mustard?"

"Nope. Already used it. She ain't give you none?"

"Naw, these bitches tryin' to fuck over me. Mad 'cause I 'm such a beast on the stick-and-move tip."

"Oh, you was fightin' the police?"

"Man, dig this here: I beat the brakes off two of them fat bastards. I just gave up 'cause I knew they was gon' shoot me if I mashed it on 'em too thick."

Marlon's fictitious tales were interrupted when the turnkey came back. "Hill, Marlon Hill."

"Yo! What's poppin'? My broad down here to bail me out?"

The turnkey held her laugh as she asked, "You mean the one who put the PPO out on you?"

"Oh, naw. Fuck her. I meant one of my other broads."

"No one came for you. How much money do you have with you?"

"I had two gees', but them police stole it!"

"Do you want to file a complaint?"

"Naw, it ain't nothin' to me; they can have it."

"Well, your twenty-three hours are up. You're being released on personal bond. They have your paperwork with your court date up front."

As Marlon walked out of his cell, he peeked over to say farewell to his neighbor. He stood speechless as he watched the guy in the cell walk over to the bars.

"What's up Marlon?"

E. Scrill/DRUG LORDS

"Jay! I thought you said your name was Smooth? What you in here for?"

"A bunch of tickets. I'll be out soon as I see the judge. So Mack ain't over there no more?"

"Naw. He bounced. I got the block doin' twenty-five hun a day. Holla at me when you get out," Marlon said. This time his lies were not to seem like a big shot, but to bait a vengeful trap. He knew Jay's reputation, and knew the sound of twenty-five hundred dollars would surely get him to go to the flat and do what Marlon couldn't.

*   *   *

Fleetwood checked his pager which was already overflowing with calls. The address appeared on the screen for the house where he was to deliver the dose of capsules.

He had been going to the victim's homes since Mack didn't have enough capsules yet to open shop full blast. He didn't mind delivering except for the fact that most of the stops were in the suburbs where the police would be quick to pull him over for being black.

After he made the transaction in Dearborn, he tossed the large stack of bills onto the passenger seat and pulled off.

As Fleet wheeled down Michigan Avenue, his heart pumped at light speed as he noticed a police cruiser in his rear view mirror. He knew if he got pulled over and they discovered the large sum of cash, he would be ripped off and possibly stomped silly.

He sighed deep as the cruiser turned off. He thought of the twenty-thousand he made taxing the victims two grand a pop, and knew that he couldn't ever go back to the dirty bag of dope he worked so many years. He decided to spend some of his take on Mack, even though he knew Mack was getting five gees' from every sale.

After putting up Mack's cash, Fleetwood went to see his jeweler; to have a masterpiece created, just to show how much he appreciated the opportunity to work the clean sack of

155

dope. He had no idea exactly what he was going to have made, knowing that Mack already had more gold and diamonds than a pirate, but knew it would have to be something unique.

*   *   *

Ray sat beside Mack on his living room sofa. For the last few days she had been trying to find a way to tell her father what she had done with the capsules that he left in her room.

"What's on your mind?" Mack asked. "You look like you're thinking about changing the grades on your report card so mommy don't beat that ass."

"Well, since you asked, I guess it is a grown-up version of that. My father is gon' wonder where his medicine is pretty soon, and I don't know what the hell I'm gon' tell him."

"You mean the stuff you gave to me?"

"Yeah. The first time I told him it was for a friend of mine, so that's no problem. But, that last stuff I was just supposed to be keeping for him till he needed it."

"And let me guess...you gave it to me to help me out?"

Ray tried to hide her blush as she rolled her eyes at Mack.

"Aww, that's so cute. She got in twuble tryin' to help her man," Mack joked while smothering her cheek with a flurry of kisses.

Ray stuck an elbow into Mack's gut. "It ain't funny. You should be the one to help me out."

Mack straightened up, "Don't even worry about it."

"What you mean, don't worry? He trusted me, and I did what I wanted to. I just feel like I played him."

"You ain't play him. Look, tell me everything about that situation with the stuff."

"I told you, he invented the stuff and was tryin' to find a way to sell it without gettin' discovered by anyone."

"He live in ATL, right?"

156

"Yeah."

"Aw, man! I just realized what is really goin' on; you played that man out of his shit!"

"See, you playin' games. I should've known you was gon' do me like this. Now, I guess it's my problem, huh?"

"Well, baby, you did it, not me."

Ray felt like slapping Mack for making jokes after she stressed her relationship with her father for him. "You ain't like I thought you was gon' be, you know that?"

"Now hold up! I could maybe help you, but you gotta be extra, extra nice to me. I mean you gotta be…naw, that's okay, you ain't ready!"

Ray watched Mack's eyes as he talked. He was taking in all of her curves in the tight-fitting skirt she had on. The whole time his dick was growing in his jogging pants. *He just want some pussy.*

"Yeah, see, if I help you, then you gotta help me," he continued as Ray moved toward him.

Ray felt herself getting wet, possibly due to a sudden hormone surge because of her momentary anger. She reached under her skirt and pulled down her thong while Mack sat and stared like a big freak. She popped the panty--rubber-band style--at his head.

"See there, that wasn't nice. I knew you wasn't ready for my help."

Ray pulled the drawstring loose on his jogging pants, holding in her laugh because he never bothered to remove the thong from the top of his head.

"Is that nice?" she asked as she smothered his veiny dick with her coochie.

"Oh, that's nice! Nice indeed!"

"How nice?" Ray asked as she watched Mack's eyes close.

"Nice and sweet. Sweet as sugar. That's why you my Sugar Ray," he moaned.

"So, you gon' help your Sugar Ray, right?"

E. Scrill/DRUG LORDS

"Oh, hell yeah! I got you."

After sex, Ray took a relaxing bubble bath with Mack. He told her he had a way to smooth things out, and for her not to worry. So she didn't.

She watched as he dressed in a denim, I.N.K. short set and stuffed a duffel bag full of bankrolls. He then told her to use the bathroom so she could take a ride with him.

Ray watched the scenery as they cruised down I-75. She was feeling a buzz from a joint she smoked with Mack. The warm night air coupled with the smooth jazz that was playing had her feeling relaxed and stress-free. She began to doze.

"Ray, wake up," Mack said. You got to use the bathroom?"

Ray stretched and looked around. They were at a truck stop somewhere. The digital clock on the dashboard read three-thirty a.m.

"Where we at?" she wanted to know.

"Kentucky."

"What? Where the hell you goin'?"

"ATL. You goin'?"

"Well shit, it don't look like I got much of a choice."

"Fine as you is, I doubt that any of these truckers will have a problem with you gettin' in with them."

"Ha-ha. What are you going to Atlanta for, Mack?"

"To see your father. What else?"

"What? Hold up! We can't just go down there like that. He's already gon' kill me. Then it's not like you and him are the best of friends."

"Chill out. Go pee. We only got five more hours to go. I got all the money I made off the stuff with me. I'm gon' give it to him and see what happens. Either he is gon' make me a partner, or, well, that's yo' ass!"

"You crazy, you know that?" Ray stomped to the restroom…praying.

Chapter 18

Mack watched Ray walk up the cobblestone walkway to her father's front door. Mack thought about how serene the area was and knew for a fact that he wasn't in the 'hood anymore. He would have no problem with the long drive to Atlanta, just as long as he could slang the cure, he was cool with whatever.

After Ray had been inside for a few minutes, she stuck her head out the door and waved Mack in.

"How's it going, Mackenzie?" Dr. Fluellen asked. "Ray told me that you two had something to discuss with me, and that she wouldn't do it without you. So, being a man of my age, we might as well get to the point. When's the due date?"

"Due date?" Ray asked with her hand on her hip. "I ain't pregnant. Don't burn no bread on me; I ain't ready to be no mother yet."

"Well, what is so important that you two had to drive eight hundred miles unannounced to talk to me about?" He turned to Mack. "You want to ask for Rachel's hand in marriage?"

Mack was on front street. He looked Dr. Fluellen in

159

the eye, but could see Ray in his peripheral vision, watching, fully alert. *I bet she just love this shit!* "Well, not exactly."

"Daddy, I gave the stuff you left to Mack, and he sold it. But, before you get mad you should know that I care a lot for him, and I wanted to help him."

Mack could see that the news came as a shock to Dr. Fluellen. As the older man deliberated, Mack's speedy heartbeat felt like a racehorse galloping in his chest. He felt like he couldn't move; as if he were cemented up to his chin by the thick tension in the room.

Mack could see that Ray was on edge from the waiting also. She began fidgeting with her necklace.

"Ray, I told you not to tell anyone about this stuff!" her father finally began. "This may be worse than any situation this guy was ever into. What was it that he needed help with anyway?"

"Well, sir…I was a drug dealer," Mack interjected, feeling that he should be the one to tell of his dirty deeds. "But, since Ray gave me that stuff, I left all that alone. I was hoping that we could work together to help the less fortunate." Mack tried his best to speak proper English, but could feel the ghetto slang yearning to spill from his lips.

He was completely out of pocket trying to get down with another brother's hustle. He was always the one calling the shots, not waiting to see if he could work someone else's bag. He felt almost as if he were on some kind of job interview, and wished he had on a suit and tie.

"So, you found yourself a thug, huh?" Dr. Fluellen asked to Ray.

"Now, Daddy…"

Sounds like a no to me. Oh shit, the money! Mack thought as he ran out the door.

"See, Daddy," he could hear Ray saying before the door closed behind him.

Mack took his time walking back up the walk, hoping that when he got back in the house he could get an earful of the doctor telling Ray how he really felt about the whole thing. He pulled the door open and went back inside.

"...And what did he do with the money he made anyway; blow it all on jewelry and speakers for that truck?" Dr. Fluellen asked Ray.

"Naw," Mack said, scrapping the proper speech, deciding to let his nuts hang a little since he now had something to work with. "I got the scratch right here. I feel like it's yours 'cause you never said I could have the medicine anyway." Mack hoped his gesture would prove to the doctor that he would be loyal and wasn't a fuck up. If nothing else, he hoped the duffel bag would at least put the doctor in a better mood.

"How much did you make off the stuff anyway?" Dr. Fluellen asked.

"The ticket was five gee's a pop, so multiply that by fifteen." Mack unzipped the bag and put the cheddar in the doctor's view. He watched as the doctor's eyes bloated with money hunger. *Got him! Probably so used to credit cards yo' ass never saw that much cheese in one place before,* Mack reasoned as he watched the doctor try to suppress a greedy grin.

"You say five grand a pop, huh?"

"Yup! I chose that price 'cause I figured most people with good sense could come up with it to save their life, and for those who can't, they would be too much of a security risk to deal with anyway."

"Oh, I see you're cautious about security, huh? Well that's good. That's good. Tell you what...I'll think about everything while I count all this up. It's only eight-thirty, and you two woke me. I got company upstairs. Make yourselves at home; the fridge is full, so you can make breakfast if you want. I'm going down to my lab."

"But tell me," Mack began. "How do you feel about the price I charged? Too low?"

"Oh no! Not at all!"

161

E. Scrill/DRUG LORDS

After watching the grinning doctor disappear around the corner, Mack twisted his lips and nodded his head triumphantly toward Ray. "I told you," he mouthed.

Ray flashed her tits.

*   *   *

"I'm gon' put somebody else downstairs to work," Mack told Angelique. "This new thang we workin' with is goin' like hotcakes. I want you to keep a back-up sack up here with you in case we run out down there and I'm not around." He tossed Angelique a thousand dollars in small bills for her participation.

"You ain't 'bout to go yet, are you? I was hoping we could play a little."

Mack loved the way Angelique looked in her red nightie, but was burnt-out from the celebratory fucks Ray gave him at the truck stops in every state on the way home from ATL for handling the situation with her father with such finesse. That didn't include the goodies he had coming for his escape from the crack game.

Mack now had two shoe boxes full of medicine that the doctor had agreed to take forty grand a box for.

"Maybe when I bring the work through. I'm tired as hell right now."

Mack stopped by the seafood store to check with Faye, to see if she was still down with the program.

"Hey, Mack. You right on time; I need a ride home."

Mack kicked it with Faye about helping him out while he drove her about a mile to her home. He noticed what looked like Weasel's car backing out of her driveway.

"That's your crib?" he asked.

"Yeah. That's my brother, Weasel. He probably 'bout to go scoop one of his hood rats."

"I ain't know you had a brother."

"Yeah. It's just me and him."

"Well, hit me up later so we can kick it some more."

162

E. Scrill/DRUG LORDS

Weasel blew his horn, but Faye thought it was for her and didn't see Mack nod his head to Weasel as she waved. She got out and ran into the house. Mack followed Weasel.

Chapter 19

"Hello, Johnny? This Mack. Where you at? Cool! You and Ross get over here to the drug store on Livernois and Ewald Circle. Weasel just pulled in here and he 'bout to get in my truck to holla at me. Naw, he don't know Ninean is my sister, or that that was Stan's spot they robbed. So when y'all get here, snatch him up after I pull off."

"What's up dog?" Weasel asked as he got into Mack's truck. Mack passed the joint he was smoking without saying a word.

"Damn, this some bomb-ass shit," Weasel choked.

"So, what you been up to?" Mack asked.

"Shit, man. Just tryin' to get my money right. Had to let ol' boy go I was with that day at Marlon's."

"What went down?"

"Dude was just fowl, that's all."

"But, why you say that?"

"You remember how he had Marlon's girl; 'bout to rape her and shit? Well, I met this chick at the casino and took her to the room so I could hit it."

"I'm listenin'."

"Well, after I hit it, I went to get some blunts and shit,

164

and left him at the room with her. I gets back to find her
raped, and all my loot gone."

"Straight up?"

"Yeah. I ain't seen him since, but when I do, I got
somethin' for that ass!"

*Damn, maybe this fool didn't even rape 'Nean. He was
just dumb enough to leave my sister alone wit' that nigga. But
that still don't mean he ain't stick up Stan's joint. I might need
to use his ass to find the other fool, though.* "Gon' fuck him up,
huh?"

"Man, hell yeah! I was diggin' that chick I was with,
but after that bullshit jumped off, who could blame her for not
wanting to fuck with me no more."

"Well dig, I got some major shit I'm puttin' together.
You wanna work?"

"I'm ready to twerk, baby!"

"I hear you talkin'. I'm gon' see just how ready you
are. I'm gon' let you run this joint I'm 'bout to crank up. We
ain't slangin' crack or none of that other shit, so you can't tell
nobody 'bout it."

"I don't talk."

"Matter of fact, if you get down, you gotta stay there
till we through with the bag."

"You mean locked-up in the spot like y'all used to do
them young niggas back in the day?"

"It's not just keepin' you in; it's keepin' other
mu'fuckas out, too. It ain't like you gon' be no hostage or
nothin'. Shit, you gon' be gettin' a gee a week. Maybe even
fifteen hundred once we get poppin'."

"The bread sound good, but I don't know 'bout bein'
locked-up in no hot-ass spot."

Mack watched as Ross and Johnny pulled up next to
Weasel's car. Ross had his seat tilted all the way back so
Weasel couldn't see his face.

"Remember, we ain't sellin' 'cain or weed so the po-
pos won't be comin' unless somebody rat us out. You ain't

165

gotta worry 'bout stick-up men; they can't get in. We on a whole new page. You gon' thank me later for puttin' you down with this new bag."

"So, it ain't dope?"

"It's not that kind of dope. This some other shit."

"Kinda like that synthetic 'cain or something', huh?"

"Kinda-sorta, but not really. Look, I gotta go. You gon' work or what?"

"I'll try the shit out for a while, man, but I just don't like bein' locked-up."

"Dig, I'm gon' have yo' sister bring you everything you need while you there; you gon' be straight."

"How long you been fuckin' wit' sis?"

"Man, I ain't never touch her." *Yet!*

"Well, that's on y'all anyway. Might as well work the joint; I'm broke as hell. When you gon' be ready?"

"I'll have your sis get in touch with you. But, more than likely, tomorrow. Let me holla at my mans right there," Mack said pointing at Johnny.

"Oh, they with you? I ain't know who them niggas was. Holla when you ready. I'm 'bout to go get with this little breezy."

"Use a rubber!"

Mack went over to fill Johnny and Ross in on the turn-around. They were pissed at the thought of losing out on the dope and sticky weed that was on Weasel's head.

* * *

Marlon strolled down Davison Avenue with Count Basie. Marlon was trying to scope out the rear of the flat to see if Angelique had Mack or any other guys over, but he could see nothing in the upper window except the light from the television.

"Man, I'm tired of walkin' back and forth," The Count began. "You need to just go over there and tell her you want her back. That ain't hard. First, you better chew some gum,

166

'cause it smell like you got a dragon in yo' mouth."

"Fuck you, nigga."

"I'm just sayin, you need to douche yo' throat or somethin'. You know it got to be bad if I can smell it and we outside."

"Why you always got to fuck with me when I'm tryin' to think?"

"Well, if that's what you doin, I wish you would close yo' mouth while you do."

"Let's get back to your crib so we can hit this bump I got."

"What about the nigga you supposed to meet over here?"

"Don't look like he gon' show up. Ain't shit goin' on over there anyway."

"Maybe he smelled that hot-ass breath and said fuck it."

"Will you shut the fuck up!"

"I ain't gon' keep comin' to help you if you gon' be actin' like that, nigga."

"I'm straight on yo' help. A nigga can't even think with you around."

"Did you ever think that maybe the nigga you lookin' for is in there playin' hide-the-salami with your baby girl?"

"I hate you!"

After smoking with the Count, Marlon decided to crack on him for a place to sleep.

"Marlon, you know you my main man, but that might cause problems with me and my sweet thang. And another thang, I hope you don't take this personal either, but I don't let no niggas around my baby."

Marlon thought of his own situation and knew just where Basie was coming from. The wise words troubled him, but still he left without saying a word; feeling like a complete asshole.

        *   *   *

167

Mack looked at Faye as she thought about being the one to run the dope to his new spot. He knew she would accept, but was trying to stall with her answer so that she wouldn't sound too desperate. Since no money was discussed, Mack knew that she would more than likely take whatever he gave her. He had no plans of taking advantage of her, though. He knew that if things got hot, the first ones to rat to the cops would be those who felt like they got played during the operation. But, at the time that the operation was in play, they would never stop what they were doing for fears that things might get better, then they would lose out. But, once shit gets hot, they give up info in alphabetical order. Mack knew that snitches couldn't always be fully avoided, even if he treated everyone good. But, if he treated them right, and they still told, then he knew he could handle his business without having a guilty conscience.

"So, how am I supposed to get way over there to the spot anyway?" Faye asked. "You know my care is broke."

Mack deliberately placed Weasel in the new spot, which was actually the property he obtained from Big Stan, to keep Faye from coming in contact with Angelique. The move would also put Weasel in a foreign environment. "Use your brother's. He won't need it; he'll be too busy."

"He ain't gon' let me touch his funky little car."

"I'll kick it with him."

"I still don't know why you ain't tell me you knew him when you dropped me off the other day."

'Cause you on a need-to-know-basis. "You ain't ask."

The conversation stopped as the two listened to a news brief over the radio. "...And in world news...The U.S. has stopped all incoming flights from Haiti and South Africa, due to the large amount of ZGP infected passengers..."

"Them dirty muthafuckas know they doctored that shit up," Mack said.

"I wish I had a cure for that shit; I would get paid

sellin' it," said Faye.

"Ain't no cure," Mack said, knowing he would never even tell her exactly what she was transporting. He grabbed the back of Faye's head and steered it to his crotch. She didn't hesitate to get busy once he whipped-out. *Damn, I guess I was sleepin' on you; you got mad skills!*

*   *   *

Marlon decided to check with Rose to see if he could chill at her crib for the night. He walked past his old flat to see if there was any activity. He crossed the street to avoid walking past a hooded figure coming toward him.

"Marlon," the figured called out.

Marlon froze, waiting for the stranger to reveal his identity. He crossed the street in Marlon's direction.

"Where you goin'?"

"Jay! Man, what the hell took you so long?"

"I rode by here twice, but you was with somebody."

"That was my dog; he cool."

"I don't ever let nobody that's not involved know when I'm 'bout to do some dirt. That always cuts down on the snitch factor. Feel me?"

"I feel you."

"Man, it don't look like shit goin' down at this joint. I thought you said you had it doin' thousands every day?"

"It was. After I got knocked, I guess everybody got scared to fall through."

"Naw, you on some bullshit! Fiends gon' keep comin' if you got some A-1 shit!"

"I ain't bullshittin'. Listen, these other niggas 'bout to come through here and set up. I'm tellin' you, they handlin' major weight. I can't take 'em by myself, that's why I need you."

"And you say they from the east side?"

"Yeah. You got to plug them fools when you rob them, too."

"What about your girl?"

"Fuck that bitch! She probably fuckin' one of them niggas right now. You might have to plug her ass, too; you know she know yo' face."

"I got that. I'm gon' wait till I see the custos come back. That way I know they got work in there with 'em."

Chapter 20

Fleetwood's pager was overflowing. He never thought he would get such a response for the cure by just word of mouth. Angelique had not been out scouting for new customers since they ran out of medicine.

Knowing that there was no more medicine, he called Mack anyway to give him the gift he had made for him.

"Hey, what's up, Fleet?" Mack asked.

"I'm just callin' to holla at you. You wanna grab a drink or a bite to eat?"

"That sounds cool. Meet me at Starter's."

Fifteen minutes later, they grabbed a booth at the small eatery and ordered Coronas while they waited for their T-bones to come.

"I got a little somethin' for you," Fleetwood said, pulling a white-gold charm from his pocket.

"This is fresh as hell, but what is it?"

"It's called a caduceus. It is used as the symbol for the medical profession. I thought it would only be right for you to have one since you're actually the one doing all the curing around here. The snake's eyes are sapphires, and the rest is white-gold. I didn't even bother with a chain 'cause I know you already got a bunch of them."

"Man, this is cold! Good lookin' out."

"Just a little somethin' to show you I appreciate you puttin' me down with the new bag. I know ain't nothin' poppin' right now, but I still had a nice little run while you was holdin'."

"You ready to get busy again?"

"What? It's back in effect?"

"All day!"

"Hell yeah! My pager been blowin' up. What we workin' wit' this time?"

"I got that spot I was tellin' you about ready for you. I want you to work with Johnny and Ross, though. They'll take care of business."

"Okay, if you say so. I'll just toss them young niggas the last of the 'cain I had. They'll love that. Just as long as they got some chips to grab some gym shoes and rims, they cool."

"Make sure you stack all your bread 'cause I don't know how long we gon' be in business. But, right now, it's all the way live."

Fleet's mind flashed on the thousands he made from the last batch of capsules, and knew from the way Mack talked that there would be much more to come. Back in the day, Fleetwood knew from the way Mack handled himself that he would never regret taking the youngster under his wing. He knew Mack had potential, but would have never guessed that young Mack would manifest and be the one to help him leave illegal drugs alone. *Life is good!* He downed the rest of his brew.

*   *   *

Jay had been watching the flat for nearly a week and saw no signs of traffic. He even sent a few dopefiends to the window to see if anyone was there, but they never got an answer at the window.

E. Scrill/DRUG LORDS

He parked down the block one night to watch the house and finally saw someone going up the driveway. *Hell yeah! They back in business!* He had been sitting with his car running for so long that he forgot to check his fuel gauge. He tried to pull off and ride by to see if he recognized the person going to the flat's backyard, but his car stalled in the middle of the street. *Shit! I don't believe this shit!*

After walking two blocks to the gas station, Jay returned with a gas can and emptied it into his tank. He noticed people from two different cars walking up the driveway to the flat, but figured he better drive back to the gas station to fill up before he staked the place out any further.

Jay had lucrative thoughts dancing around in his head. He knew that if the new dealers were as major as Marlon had said, he would know for sure once he had them hog-tied. He figured that Marlon was just mad that he got ran out of his spot, and didn't really care about getting any of the money from robbing the new dope men. *Payday! And I ain't givin' Marlon ho-ass shit! That fool is too scared to even scope the joint out with me. Ain't no way I'm gon' split my dough with a bitch-ass nigga like that! And I hope that little bitch he had is still there, 'cause I got some unfinished business with her.*

In the gas station, Jay paid for his gas, but noticed that the man that went in front of him had burnt fingertips like a crackhead. He was scrawny and had nappy hair. Jay hurried out the door to catch him so that he could send him to the dope spot to see just what was going on. "Hey, my man! Let me holla at you!"

"What's the deal?" the suspected dopefiend asked as he walked toward Jay. "You need your gas pumped or something?"

"Oh yeah. You can handle that for me."

"They call me, Count Basie."

"Okay, cool. You wanna do me another favor? I'll take care of you."

"Talk to me."

173

"It's a spot down the street. I want you to go over there and buy a rock for me. You can have it if you want after you get it. Just tell me if you know any of the people in there and how many of them it is. Cool?"

"Look, Mr. Officer, I ain't done nothin' wrong. Why y'all gotta mess with ol' Basie?"

"Look, my man, I'm not the police. I'm just tryin' to see who's in there, that's all."

"I know who in there already."

"Who."

"My mellow, Marlon."

"No he ain't."

"Oh, you know him?"

"Yeah, that's my dog."

"Oh, that must've been you he was waitin' for that night."

"Yeah, that's right. So you must know what happened over there, huh?"

"I only heard bits and pieces. But hey, it's gon' be two dollars for pumpin' the gas. Now give me the ten so I can go cop."

Jay drove back to his spot down the block and let Basie walk back to the flat.

He watched the Count pop his collar as he went up the driveway. Fifteen minutes had passed and Jay saw no signs of the Count. He figured Marlon was playing some kind of sick game, and had let the Count in when he went to cop. Jay hopped out and started toward the flat.

In the backyard, Jay stood in line behind a man in a casual outfit. The guy knocked on the window, which was boarded up, then a small section of the board came unplugged from the inside. An eye peeped out of the small hole.

"What's the deal?" the owner of the eye asked.

The man in front of Jay jammed a large wad of cash into the hole.

Aww shit! These niggas movin' weight outta this bitch!

174

E. Scrill/DRUG LORDS

Hell yeah! Time to get my shit and go up in this muthafucka!
Jay walked away as the man that was in front of him still stood
there. As he walked past the side door, he noticed that it was
now cracked. It wasn't when he first walked up.

As he took his next few steps, Jay felt a sharp pain in
the back of his head. The ground started moving closer and
closer to his face in what seemed like slow motion. At the
same time, he began experiencing tunnel-vision. *That damn
Count!* he thought as everything went black.

*   *   *

Angelique heard seven knocks coming from the ceiling
downstairs. That meant that the men dealing out of the lower
flat needed more drugs. She grabbed one of the five remaining
paper bags and headed down the steps.

Mack had left twenty of the lunch-sized bags that were
full of smaller plastic baggies. In each plastic baggy were
dozens of capsules. She didn't know what kind of drug the
capsules were, but knew that they seemed to move much faster
than the crack that Marlon sold months before. The workers
ran through fifteen of the twenty bags Mack left in two days.
And all of the customers that came for the baggies seemed to
be well-off, unlike the dusty crackheads that staggered up the
driveway day and night to see her ex.

Mack's new workers didn't seem like the type of guys
that would be caught dead in a drug house. They were neat
and clean-shaven; like him.

One of the men, John Dollar, as he called himself,
would try to holla at her every time she responded to their
knocks. Under normal circumstances she would have given
him a play, but not while she was fucking the boss.

"Damn, I ain't think you would look that good when
you first wake up," Johnny began. "You don't even look like
you get morning breath."

"Yeah, whatever. Here's the stuff."

"You hungry?"

175

"Why? What's up?"

"Well, if you were, I was gon' say I'll buy us some of that seafood over there if you'll go swoop it up."

"I'll go; I really ain't doin' nothin' else."

"Bet! Hey, while you waitin' for the food to get ready, hit the store on the corner and grab us a six-pack." Johnny gave her a fifty. "Keep the change."

"Let me run upstairs an put on my shoes."

As Angelique started through the vacant lot toward the seafood spot, she felt like she was being watched. She turned to see a pair of eyes watching her from the hole in the board that covered the window.

"I'm just watching to make sure don't nobody grab you, that's all," Johnny 's voice said through the hole.

Yeah, I bet. She tried to pull her shirt down to cover her behind. She giggled to herself when she heard Johnny yell, "I can still see it!"

Angelique got the food and started across the street when she saw what looked like Marlon, talking to a couple of narcotics officers. She looked back again and saw him getting into their unmarked car.

That dumb-ass musta got caught-up!

Later that evening, she peeked out the front window to watch the monotonous trickle of customers walking up the driveway like she usually did when she got bored, and saw the unmarked police car creeping past the flat.

She speed-dialed Mack to put him up on game.

Chapter 21

Mack was running through the new cure like a fool ran through money. He and his crew pushed a full shoe box to victims in less than a week. With the capsules going at that rate, he knew he would have to employ a driver to recop for him every week. That would be the only way to keep both spots cranking.

He knew he needed someone who was dependable and also had a good driving record in case they got pulled over along the way. This someone would have to be the kind of person the authorities would never suspect of drug trafficking due to the risk of exposing the cure. The list for qualified individuals was not long at all.

He couldn't think of sending Ray. Two days every week without her would be too much. There was no way he was going to put that much distance between him and her gold-lined twat. Then too, he couldn't have her father thinking that she was being used; she was definitely not a candidate.

He knew he would flip the capsules quick, but word of mouth had his spots off the hook. And Angelique told him that more and more out of state license plates were coming through. Mack had the game on lock. No one on the planet could get right unless they paid him. If things kept flowing like they were, he would soon have people flying in from China.

I got this goin', but I need a runner. If Ray's daddy wasn't my plug, I could send one of these ho's I'm fucking with.

Ninean walked through the door with a bag of groceries. "Mack didn't you say you was gon' give me some money to go shopping?"

"You need some money?"

"I always need money."

"You wanna make a gee a week?"

"Doin' what?"

"Drivin' to ATL."

"Every week?"

"Yeah. It would be better if you did it for me, 'cause then I wouldn't have to go meet somebody out in the street to get my stuff; you would just bring it home with you."

"In my car?"

"Take mine if you want. Matter of fact, if you help me out, you can have that bitch; it's time for me to drop somethin' new anyway."

"Can I get a advance so I can go shoppin' first? I might meet one of them fine country boys; you know they be ballin' too!"

"C'mon now, sis. This shit is strictly business; that's why I'm askin' you. I need somebody dependable to get my stuff here without gettin' caught-up on the way. You gon' be goin' to see Ray's daddy to get the cure for that new shit goin' around."

"Oh shit! You workin' that now?"

"Workin' the hell out of it!"

"Okay, a gee a week. When do I start?"

"Get some rest. You can ride soon as the sun go down. That way none of them nosy-ass Ohio police can see what color you are. By the time the sun rise, you should be in

178

Kentucky."

"What's so bad about Ohio?"

Mack laughed, then said, "When crack first came out, niggas from the D went through there and burnt that bitch all the way out! I mean shit got so bad, the state boys start pullin' over Detroit License plates on G.P."

"Why didn't they just sell their dope here, where they from?"

"Rollin' out of town is like throwin' down in a drought."

"A drought?"

"When dope get tight as hell. Okay, now you had your lesson. What you tryin' to do, write a book or somethin'?"

"Shit, I could with all the wild shit y'all niggas be doin.'"

"Go get some rest so you don't get sleepy; it's ten hours to the dirty south. And make sure you use the cruise control so you don't drift over the speed limit."

"I don't like usin' that thang."

"I'm tellin' you to use that 'cause it will help in case you have to slow down. Just think of it like you're in a police car lookin' for speeders. If a car shoot by you and you see brake lights, then you know they had to stop doin' what they was doin'. And why would they have to stop doin' what they was doin' unless they was doin' somethin' wrong? Now with the cruise control, you can just speed up and slow down with the button on the steering wheel. So, use the cruise. Feel me?"

*   *   *

Mack sat on the couch with Angelique trying to see what she had to show him. She refused to tell him over the phone, only saying that she would rather him see it for himself. He knew that was an attempt to get her legs around him. Whatever it was, she could have said it over the phone. He had no problems with stickin' Angelique, but some days

179

after Ray got done with him, he didn't feel like touching another woman. Even when Ray had her panties padded-up, she made sure she sucked the life out of him before he left her.

Mack didn't know if Ray suspected him of cheating, or was just horny as hell. Whatever it was, he was loving every minute of it. Thoughts of her constantly monopolized his mind.

"See, that's what I was telling you about," Angelique said, pointing to the police car creeping with their lights off. "I saw Marlon talking to them, then they started ridin' by like every hour."

"He ratted us out! Guess we should've did it your way and busted his head. I called myself feelin' sorry for him, too." *I guess fuckin' with Ray got me goin' soft.*

"I tried to tell you. I knew somethin' was up 'cause he didn't try to sneak back over here."

"Oh, so you just think that pussy so good that he would've been out here violatin' restrainin' orders and shit, huh?"

"Shut up. I ain't say all that. I just know he was salty as hell when they whipped his ass and drug him outta here."

"I bet you was in here laughin' and shit, wasn't you?"

"Yup! So, what you gon' do about this shit? You ain't worried about the police comin' in here?"

"Don't even worry about it; I got this. I been doin' this forever. I thought you was gon' give me a manicure?" Mack tried to buy some more time to allow the cheeseburger he just ate to charge his batteries. He was trying to hang out for a while since Angelique had been complaining lately that he wasn't spending any time with her anymore.

He recently told Johnny that he could bone her if she would go for it. Mack hoped in the time that he wasn't coming around that she would tramp-out and give Johnny a taste, but she seemed to be stuck like glue.

Mack shushed Angelique after hearing strange sounds coming through the vent.

180

E. Scrill/DRUG LORDS

"You hit him too hard, man. I ain't trying to kill him yet," Johnny's voice echoed up through the vent.

Next, Mack heard someone moaning in what sounded like excruciating pain. *Oh shit! These hot-ass niggas puttin' the hurt on somebody! It's too hot over here for this shit. I knew I should've made Fleet stay over here.*

Mack ran down the steps to the basement where he found Johnny, Ross, and someone on the floor hog-tied with a pillow case over his head.

"What the fuck y'all doin'?" Mack asked.

Both Ross and Johnny jumped at the sound of Mack's voice like a little boy caught with his fingers in his sister's change purse. They couldn't have known Mack was in the flat since Angelique let him in through the front door that time. "Man we caught this nigga creepin' 'round back," Ross began. "He was tryin' to get us!"

"Who is it?"

"Jay!" Johnny said.

"Well, you can't keep him here; five-o is out there creepin'."

"The fifties?"

"That's what I said. Why didn't y'all tell me he was here?"

"I was tryin' to ask him where my car was," Johnny said.

"Fuck that car! You can always get another one. Marlon got us hot as hell right now! I ain't tryin' to get knocked right now, and if they run up in here and catch that mu'fucka tied-up, that's a kidnappin' charge."

"So, what, just let him go?" Johnny asked with his face creased with disappointment.

"Naw, he ain't gettin' away this time. I need y'all to go work the other spot right now. I got a better plan."

As Ross walked by Jay, he kicked him in the head and acted like he tripped.

*   *   *

Mack moved Angelique to the new spot with Johnny and Ross. He didn't think she would mind since she would be in the upper part of the house while they dealt out of the side door and chilled in the basement. Mack had to scare her some by telling her how fierce the police were going to run up in the spot, and that she would be much safer at the new joint since it was just opened and Marlon knew nothing of it. Mack hoped that the new situation would also give Johnny a better chance to get his bone-on since he had better access to Angelique.

Mack knew Ross didn't care one way or the other; he might bang her if she gave him the green light, but wouldn't pursue her. Johnny on the other hand, would hound her constantly, and if that didn't work, he would come out of pocket…if she was down.

With the trio situated in the new spot, Mack shot Weasel over to the hot spot where Jay was still bound and gagged in the basement. Mack knew that it wouldn't be long before the authorities came in with the customers flocking in like they were.

Mack went to the upstairs flat and turned the radio up loud, but not so loud that it would bug the neighbors. Just loud enough to keep Weasel from hearing Jay in case he started moaning through his gag. With the door locked, Mack doubted that Weasel would try to jimmie the lock in order to go snooping. Mack told Weasel that he moved him because he trusted him more now.

With the flat nearly out of capsules, Mack decided not to restock it for a week or so until he saw how the police were going to act. He told Fleetwood to keep sending people just to keep the traffic up, and when they called back pissed-off, to send them to the new spot. Mack also let Faye know about the move so she could bring Weasel food and whatever he needed.

Mack went home to count his money.

Chapter 22

FBI Special Agent, Todd Schultz looked to his partner, Special Agent, Mark Brown, and asked, "Are you sure they said these monkeys are selling the cure for ZGP out of a dope house?"

"That's what they said, Schultz."

"Well, how the hell could those knuckleheads get their hands on something like that?"

"That's why we were called in; it's our job to find that out."

The two Caucasian agents surveilled the flat from a van parked down the block.

"Damn, Brown, will you look at all that fucking traffic! I bet these guys are making a million bucks a week. Now let me get this straight: we don't arrest anyone; this is just a raid to gather intelligence, right?"

"Yep. I still can't believe the way the locals came across the stuff. They pulled over some guy for outstanding warrants, then he just started squealing like a pig. That was some lucky fluke!"

"Yeah, but the worst part about the whole thing, is that the unlucky fuck still got hauled in for his tickets."

E. Scrill/DRUG LORDS

"What an asshole!"

"There's our back-up! Get ready, we're going in!"

The special agents surrounded the flat. Agents Brown and Schultz went in through the unlocked side door. They stopped at the door of the first floor dwelling, while another set of agents quickly moved up the steps to the upper flat.

Brown twisted himself into the first-floor flat. He tiptoed with his service weapon drawn. He could hear voices from the next room.

"I don't even know no Marlon," he heard a male voice say, then continue with, "This my shit now. This ain't no crack house either. I'm much bigger than that now. Look, you can just leave if you ain't with the program; closed mouths don't get fed!"

Brown waved his partner around him, through the doorway, while he covered him. Brown heard the other agents kicking in the door to the upstairs flat.

Brown watched as his partner neared the black male that stood in front of a kneeling female. The male had his pants down around his knees. Brown could feel his adrenaline surging through his system.

"Don't move! Government agents! Put your hands on your head! You…female! Get down on the floor!"

After the remaining capsules were seized, Weasel was seated in a chair and interrogated. His female friend, Rose, was taken to a separate room to have her brains picked.

Brown offered Weasel a smoke. "So you say you don't know what this stuff is, huh?"

"Naw, man! I ain't even know that shit was here!"

"We overheard you telling the lady that this was your operation. Just what kind of an operation do you have going on here?"

Brown's questions were interrupted when one of the other agents stuck his head around the corner. "Brown, can I speak to you for a minute?"

Brown stepped into the next room with the agent.

184

E. Scrill/DRUG LORDS

"We aren't getting anything out of the guy we found tied-up in the basement; he won't even give us a name."

Brown rubbed his chin, then said, "Don't worry about him. Leave him tied up. Me and my partner will take things from here."

Brown waited until the other agents cleared the house, then spoke with his partner in the kitchen. "Well, it doesn't look like we'll find out much from these guys. I don't know the story on the one in the basement, but I say we just send in the other team and let them handle it; they're better equipped for this type of thing. I want to get back to my regular duties, and look for terrorists. These street punks are way outta my league."

"Yeah, you're right. I don't like any of this crap. We can turn in the capsules, then just let the big guys figure out the rest."

The two agents left Weasel, Rose, and Jay handcuffed while they went back to their van. "This is Brown. We have the location secure; send in the black team."

*   *   *

Ninean walked into the house with Mack's package under her arm. She couldn't wait to see him. He had promised to let her take his truck for the trips to Atlanta, but had her driving rental cars. She hated the small cars he rented.

"Damn, 'Nean! What took so long? You was supposed to be here yesterday. And where did you get that necklace?"

"Oh, Donny wanted me to stay the night…just so he could show me around a bit. He bought me this chain. You like it?"

"Who the hell is Donny?"

"Ray's father. You ain't know his name?"

"Yeah, Mr. Fluellen."

"Well, he told me Donny. And he is very nice."

"Ray's daddy been tryin' to squeeze you?"

Ninean put her hand on her hip. "And what's wrong

185

with that? He knows how to treat a bitch, I know that much!'"

Ninean watched as Mack held his stomach in a laughing fit. She didn't like the fact that her brother found her fling funny. He was always the one with someone he could spend quality time with, and now that she found someone to make her happy, he found it funny.

"When you gon' let me use that truck like you said? You been promisin' me that since I started drivin' down there. I hate them little-ass rentals!"

"Okay, okay, hold up! Ha-ha!"

"I hate you!" Ninean stormed up to her room to call Donny.

*   *   *

Mack left the Cadillac dealership in his new Seville. He loved the way it gripped the street as he bent corners. He swooped up Ray for the maiden cruise.

She didn't say much, just kept looking through the sunroof.

Mack drove down Dexter Avenue to glimpse the traffic at the spot since he was in a new whip and no one would recognize him. He was nearly run off the road by a fire truck when his loud sound system kept him from hearing the sirens. He watched as the truck turned onto Clements.

As he drove by, he saw firefighters surrounding the flat with hoses spraying streams of water at the aggressive flames leaping from his money spot.

His glorious day was tarnished by feelings of disgust as he raced back to Ray's house to drop her off. He explained the situation , and told her that he had lots of stones to turn over.

Mack deflowered a wealth of traffic laws at break-neck speeds on his spin back to Clements.

He dialed Faye's number to hear her voice come screaming over the lines. "My brother is burning in the house!"

Mack parked at the seafood joint and dashed through

186

the crowd of bystanders where he saw Faye, being held back by a pair of firemen.

Mack rushed over and grabbed her from behind. "I got her," he told the firemen.
He dared not leave her at the scene for fears that his name would come out in one of her grief-filled screams. He held her like a baby, with one arm around her neck and the other under her knees, and carried her to his car.

"Weasel! Why can't they just get him out!"

Mack kept quiet. He knew he could do nothing to calm her.

"They killed him," she screamed.

"Who? Who killed him?" Mack wanted to know.

"The FBI just raided the house, then it start burnin'! I know they killed him!"

A brew of nausea bubbled inside Mack's gut. Nightmarish thoughts of him being caught in the house while scooping his cash flashed through his mind. He closed his eyes and tried to allow the whole situation to sink in.

"Take me home. I want to tell my mother about this to her face," said Faye.

Mack sat in the living room of Faye's house while she went to share the grisly details with her mother. A few moments later, he was wishing he had just stayed in the car.

It had been years since Mack witnessed a breakdown so dramatic that tears flowed from his own eyes. Faye's mother cried and screamed until she vomited. Mack pulled Faye to the side after her mother fell to the couch, and told her to call so he could handle the funeral expenses.

Just something so he would be able to sleep that night.

Chapter 23

Without the flat on Clements to work from, Mack had to push the cure from the new spot and whatever Fleetwood handled from his pager. He still moved a shoebox of capsules a week.

For Marlon's participation in the lost of the flat, Mack made sure Angelique gave a convincing statement to prosecutors about their domestic incident. He knew that Angelique didn't even have to show up in court for him to be convicted; the state would surely pick up the charges with the torn shirt as evidence.

After sliding Faye ten thousand to help with the funeral arrangements for her brother, Mack bought her a used Honda Accord. Ray got a new Cadillac.

Mack sat in the bed with Ray one morning after a night of sweaty sex. "So, do you like living with your mother?" he asked.

"It's okay. We get along pretty good. Why do you ask?"

"I was just wondering, that's all."

"Just curious, huh?"

"Yeah."

E. Scrill/DRUG LORDS

"You know my father is coming to town, right?"

"No. I haven't talked to him."

"I bet 'Nean knows."

"I bet she do, too. You think they really got somethin' goin on?"

"I sure do. You know yo' li'l sis went down there and put it on my old man."

"Naw. It's more like that old man is takin' advantage of my li'l sis." Before Mack and Ray could enjoy a laugh about their convo, Mack got a queasy feeling in his gut. Knowing he wouldn't make it to the bathroom in time, he rolled out of the bed onto his hands and knees and hurled his small meal from the night before into the trash can beside his bed.

He hated for Ray to see him throw up. When most of his stomach's contents were flushed, he still dry-heaved for a few more minutes. He could hear Ray giggling, but was too occupied to look up. He knew he looked foolish the way his body was jerking with the weird noises he was making. He heard Ray run out of the room.

When he was finally done, he held his position on his knees with sweat pouring from his face and a stream of drool containing little food particles leaking from his mouth. He felt Ray place a cool, damp cloth of relief on his neck. He raised up so that he was only on his knees. He began to feel dizzy from all the straining it took to puke.

Ray wiped his mouth with a napkin, then placed another cold face cloth on his forehead. "You okay?" she asked between her giggles.

Mack just collapsed onto the bed.

Ray brought him saltines from the kitchen, then cut on the ceiling fan as she took the trash can out of the room. He could hear her in the bathroom cleaning the trash can. *What the fuck is wrong with me? I'm glad my baby was here to take care of me. I hope I ain't catch that ZGP shit from none of them ho's I been fuckin' with. I would hate to give some shit to*

189

E. Scrill/DRUG LORDS

Ray, even if her father do got the cure! As Mack lay across the bed, the possibilities of him having ZGP became more and more real. Haunting thoughts of Faye and Angelique giving him unprotected suck-jobs racked his brain. When he first started fooling around with Angelique, he wasn't letting her put her mouth on his skin, but when he got hold of the cure, he relaxed a bit too much. Now, he seemed to be paying.

He knew he would be able to cure himself with no problem, but he would have to face the issue of Ray's infection as well. Which would certainly mean no more cure from her father, and no more toe-spreading dick rides with her.

Things had gone so far beyond just sex with her that he couldn't think of taking a breath without her in his life. And if she realized that she was infected, she would surely link her illness to him fucking other females.

Maybe I'll make her promise to give me another chance or I won't take the cure. Naw, fuck that. She might get pissed enough to let me die. What the hell? I sound worse than that young nigga she was with. I can't go out like that! Fuck it, if she wanna leave, I'll just let her go!

All thoughts of Faye and Angelique pissed Mack off.

He fell into a deep sleep, and when he woke, he and Ray went out to eat, and then rented videos for the evening. That night, after convincing himself that their relationship would soon be over, he spent every moment of their time holding and caressing Ray. By two a.m., he had sexed her four times. Each time he loved her with all his might…as if he were going off to prison in the morning to start a life sentence.

*   *   *

Marlon stood outside a liquor store on Dexter Avenue. He was watching the Count's dog while he went inside to cop a pint of gin for the two of them. He was starting to get tired of waiting. He wanted a buzz bad as hell. He had been somber and depressed all day.

Since the fire at the flat, he had no idea if Angelique

190

made it out safe or not. He was told that a female and two males perished in the blaze. He had lost everything.

He peeked inside after waiting twenty minutes. Marlon was hoping that the Count wouldn't be heartless enough to drink all the liquor inside the store while he baby-sat the mutt. He knew the Count could easily kill a pint alone.

He watched as the Count stumbled out of the store. The Count's toxic breath almost caused Marlon's eyes to water. "What the fuck took you so long, man?"

"I was kickin' it with my mellows behind the counter; they was askin' 'bout the fire."

"Where's the drink?"

"Man, I don't think you need to be drinkin' while you feelin' like that," the Count said with a look of concern on his face.

"Quit bullshittin'! You drunk the shit by yourself! You selfish as hell!"

"I just don't think you should be doin' that to yourself right now, that's all."

"Then why didn't you tell me that before I stood outside for twenty minutes watchin' the damned dog?"

The Count curled his lips into a devilish grin.

"Let's go by that spot around the corner and try to get us some credit."

Marlon's heart leaped at the thought of getting a rock, but no longer trusted the Count's friendship.

"I'm cool. You go."

"Okay, I see you still got a attitude. You know out here in these streets without me, you gon' fall off like a bad pack of heroin."

"I'll take my chances." Marlon headed in the opposite direction of the new crack house. He knew the Count wanted him to go along because the Count had a bad reputation for not paying when he owed money.

After taking the long way around, Marlon was allowed entry into the new spot. He looked around while the young dealers went to a back room to get the dope. They came back with a handful of rocks. Marlon's mouth began to water. "I get my check next week; let me owe you for three of 'em."

The youngsters looked at each other, and then looked at Marlon.

Marlon could see that they wanted to get rid of the dope, but was unsure of his credit rating. He also knew they were green as hell. "Dig, fellas, I'm good with payin' niggas back. Ask anybody."

"Somebody fronted us this dope so you better pay us. If he don't get his loot, he gon' be tryin' to fuck us up. So we gon' have to fuck you up if you bullshittin'."

"I can respect that, playa. Work with me." Marlon took the stones, then was knocked to the floor as the front door came crashing in.

"Freeze, police!"

Aw shit, a raid! Marlon was relieved to see that the officers in charge were the ones he had been working with, but they still cuffed him since he had a warrant for failing to appear for the domestic violence case with Angelique.

"Hey, why y'all got me in these tight-ass cuffs?"

"Because you're going to jail."

"After all that shit I helped y'all with? C'mon, man."

"We didn't get any credit for that bust; the Feds took over. We even made up a story about how we got the info about that dopehouse to cover your ass. You got any info we can use right now?"

"Naw, man. I don't do nothin' else."

"That's too bad. Looks like you're going down, my friend."

"Man, that stuff with my girl ain't nothin'. Just give me another chance; I promise to turn myself in in a few days."

"If the thing with your girl was all you had, we could give you a chance. But, it looks like you just got caught with some dope."

"What? This shit ain't mine! I just got here."

E. Scrill/DRUG LORDS

"But, you are here. We believe it might not be yours, but we gotta get our stripes some kinda way. See, if we charge these little punks with the dope, they'll maybe get a year of probation. You on the other hand, will get time in the joint."

"The joint? I can't go to prison!"

"You shoulda thought about that before you tried to be a dopeman."

"Hell naw! Hell naw! Y'all on some bullshit!"

"We really couldn't bullshit if you didn't give us the power to; thanks." The officers gave the youngsters loitering tickets while Marlon--despite his begging and conspiracy theories--was dragged off to the squad car. As he got into the vehicle, he noticed the Count standing across the street, saluting him by grabbing his nuts.

Chapter 24

Mack went by his remaining spot to grab his cash and leave more capsules. This time, he had Ray with him. He knew sparks would fly once Angelique saw the other woman with him--even though she already knew about her--but it would have been too much trouble to take Ray all the way back on the west-side, then make another trip to handle his biz. He didn't want anything else to do with Angelique anyway.

She was loyal to him, but Ray had his heart. Even if there was no Ray, Mack doubted that Angelique would have been able to capture the central part of him. He knew that if he and Ray made it through the rough times that were ahead, he would never again creep with another woman. But first, he would have to make it through.

As Mack pulled in front of the spot, he knew he had fouled up by bringing Ray. If for some reason he and Ray were destined to make it through him being infected, having Angelique running out of the house with a broken heart--ready to start shit--would just make matters worse. But he was there and hoped that his foolish decision wasn't about to make him sorry.

He was in his first real relationship and the situation

looked hopeless. He knew that if he had been having relationships all along, then he would know how to deal with things like this. But he came up playing pimp-daddy, and knew he would lose Ray forever with that attitude.

"What you thinkin' about?" Ray asked Mack, startling him out of his thoughts.

"Oh, nothing." He hopped out of the car and ran to the door.

Angelique stepped to him as soon as he walked in the door. "So, you in love now, huh?"

"Why you say that?" he asked, feeling as if she read his thoughts.

"It ain't hard to figure out. The last few times you came by, you was distant like your mind was somewhere else. You don't really let me touch you no more…"

"I guess I am, then."

"I know. I understand. Remember when we first hooked up? I told you that I knew you had somebody else. Remember?"

Straight up? Now that's how shit is supposed to be!

"So, you gon' just let me go?"

"What else can I do? It won't help me none if I ran out there and acted a fool in front of your woman. I still wouldn't have you." She walked over and kissed him on the cheek. "But I got you."

Mack walked down to the basement to kick it with Johnny and Ross. As he passed the side door, he knew that would be his way out. There was no way he was going to pass Angelique again on that day. But, for keeping the drama down, she definitely had a bonus coming.

"Man, I still ain't get them draws yet," Johnny told Mack.

"What you waitin' for?"

"We thought she was a freaky-deek, but she ain't. If I was her, and was stuck with that lame, Marlon, I would fuck around with a nigga gettin' money too. She ain't really a bad girl, and damn sho' won't trick with me."

"Think you got a better chance just waitin' till she open up to you, huh?"

"At least till she get over you; if she fuck with me then."

Mack took the money and left the dope. In a way, he felt kind of bad for trying to pass Angelique around like a blunt. But, he knew that if Johnny did get the draws, he wouldn't do her bad. Johnny's problem was with other guys, not women.

As Mack reached for his car's door handle, he looked back and saw Angelique standing in the window. At first he thought she was looking at him, but then he noticed she was making eye-contact with Ray. *Aw shit! I thought shit was gon' be cool!* He hopped in.

"Who was that?" Ray asked.

Mack looked to the window, and before he could answer, Johnny appeared and threw his arm around Angelique, pulling her away from the window. Mack stared at the vertical blinds swaying back and forth.

"Oh," Ray said. "How many people are in there anyway?"

"Enough."

        *   *   *

Donyale toweled off, then dressed. He was planning to take Ninean out to dinner and a movie. He was glad Mack had sent her to make his runs to Atlanta. Melinda had been doing a good job of keeping him company, but she wasn't a keeper. Not by his standards anyway.

He made sure that she understood when he told her that she made a good helper, but not a good companion for him. In the end, she was more concerned with the money she was getting for helping him with the capsules. He told her that would be no problem as long as she kept things strictly business.

E. Scrill/DRUG LORDS

He knew Pat would flip once she found out that his new flame was young enough to be their daughter, but he wasn't going to let that stop him. *She better be glad I saved her life!* The times he had been having with Ninean revived his once crucified heart. He knew he was going to do all he could to hold down Ninean if he could; even if it meant relocating.

As he walked toward Ninean's room, he thought of the divine sex they had been having, and was glad he started jogging or else he wouldn't have been able to keep up with her young ass.

He looked in the bedroom, but no Ninean. He followed the voices he heard downstairs. As he neared the bottom of the stairs, he could hear Mack's voice. "I know you ain't got no niggas up in my crib!" Mack said.

Donyale came down the last few steps.

"Daddy!" Ray said.

"Oh, it's you," said Mack.

"Yeah. I came as soon as Ray told me about your suspicions. I told her I would bring my equipment so I could test her myself."

Mack shot a regretful look at Ray. "You knew, too, huh?"

"Mack, how could I not know?"

"I was gon' talk to you, but..."

"Just let my father give me the test before you say anything."

Donyale gave Mack a stern look before he and Ray went up the steps to the bathroom.

*   *   *

Mack flopped down on the couch. He knew it was over now. He figured she was just enjoying a few last moments with him until she found out the results of the ZGP test. But, whether he was positive or not, it didn't matter. She probably knew from his guilty expression that he had been

197

cheating.

He heard footsteps coming down the stairs. His heart somersaulted.

Donyale came down first, still wearing a stern expression. "Well, she was positive," he said.

"Aw shit!" said Mack.

"What's wrong, son? It's not that bad."

"I know. But I just…" Mack looked at Ray as she came down the steps.

"You what?" she asked.

"I love you, that's all."

Donyale raised his eyebrows when he asked, "Then why would her pregnancy be so bad?"

"Pregnant?" Mack asked.

"Yeah," Ray said. "What did you think it was?"

END

Epilogue

Mack made over five million dollars selling the cure for ZGP, but after the next few months, the Federal Government saw that the cure was still being pushed on the streets, so they allowed the CDR to go public with the medication that they had to combat the illness.

After a year of sparring with the Federal Trade Commission and the Food and Drug Administration, Donyale was finally allowed to go public with his cure and market it properly. He still had the game on lock since the medication he had invented actually cured the disorder, and the other medications on the market only put the ZGP virus in a state of dormancy. For that, he received many awards and honors, including the Nobel Prize.

With more cash than the ghetto has roaches, Donyale gave Mack and Ray, as a wedding gift, an additional five million dollars. Mack bequeathed a million of his fortune to become a silent partner in Fleetwood's new business venture.

After watching a news special at the end of the year, Fleetwood saw that Victoria Secret had grossed over three and a half billion dollars for that year. He wanted in on the hustle.

He invented a female undergarment, The Fig Leaf, which made the thong obsolete, and was only available at his nationwide chain of Figtree outlets and over the internet.

Ninean moved in with Donyale and is now expecting twins.

E. Scrill/DRUG LORDS

Pat Fluellen received a hundred thousand dollars from Ray, and is now getting over her third ZGP infection.

*   *   *

Marlon sat in a window seat of the transport van leaving the Wayne County jail on his way to quarantine at Jackson prison. As the van stopped for a red light before getting on the freeway, Marlon looked into the window of a small Honda next to them. He could hear the other prisoners shout, "Look, y'all, she givin' him head in the car!"

Marlon instantly recognized Johnny's face as he maintained his gangsta lean while being sucked-off. As the light changed, Angelique raised her head from Johnny's lap and wiped her mouth. She had accepted Johnny as her new sponsor. She made eye-contact with Marlon and gave a teasing smile that tortured him for the remainder of his ride.

After Marlon left quarantine, he was sent to the Newberry Facility to get his GED, but found himself constantly victimized by the gangs of young hoodlums that roamed the yard. He was later befriended by a group of gays, and tricked out of his manhood. After being turned-out, he was the only one in his circle to give sexual favors on consignment.

He changed his name to Pie, and was transferred to Huron Valley's psychiatric facility for claiming to be five months pregnant.

200